Old-Fashioned Amish Mennonite Cookin' II

More Sugarless Favorites

This book contains more recipes which are sweetened with natural sweeteners such as honey, fructose, molasses, etc. There is also a large selection of recipes in the back of the book which are sweetened with fruit juices. Those sweetened with fructose have a note at the bottom of the recipe, telling how much sugar to use to replace the fructose, for those who desire to use sugar.

Edited by Susie Christner
Artwork by Charlene Kennell

ISBN 0-9656842-1-0

Psalms 1

Blessed is the man that walketh not in the counsel of the ungodly, nor standeth in the way of sinners, nor sitteth in the seat of the scornful.

But his delight is in the law of the Lord; and in his law doth he meditate day and night.

And he shall be like a tree planted by the rivers of water, that bringeth forth his fruit in his season; his leaf also shall not wither; and whatsoever he doeth shall prosper.

The ungodly are not so: but are like the chaff which the wind driveth away.

Therefore the ungodly shall not stand in the judgement, nor sinners in the congregation of the righteous.

For the Lord knoweth the way of the righteous: but the way of the ungodly shall perish.

Table Of Contents

Breads

Notes

_____

_____

_____

_____

_____

_____

_____

_____

_____

_____

_____

_____

_____

DOUGHNUTS

Mix: 2 cups milk, scalded   1 cup shortening

         ½ cup fructose   1 tsp. salt
Mix: 2 T. yeast   ½ cup warm water
         ½ tsp. honey
Mix: 2 eggs, beaten   1 cup mashed potatoes
         1 cup potato water

Mix all together and add 11-11½ cups flour. Let rise 2 hours. Roll out, cut with doughnut cutter, let rise and **fry in hot oil.** Coat with favorite glaze.
Note: If using sugar to replace fructose, use 1 cup.

SOUR CREAM OVEN DOUGHNUTS

2 cups bisquick   ¼ tsp. cinnamon
2 T. fructose   ½ cup dairy sour cream
½ tsp. nutmeg   1 egg

Mix all together until soft dough forms. Knead 10 times. Roll dough ½" thick. Cut with floured cutter. Place on ungreased cookie sheet. **Bake at 400 degrees 8-10 minutes.** Mix ½ cup fructose and 1 tsp. cinnamon. Immediately brush with melted butter and sprinkle with cinnamon mixture.
Note: If using sugar to replace fructose, use ¼ cup.

Trust Him when dark doubts assail thee,
Trust Him when thy strength is small.
Trust Him when to simply trust Him
seems the hardest thing to do.

CINNAMON TWISTS

½ cup water   1 pkg. yeast
¾ cup sour cream, lukewarm   2 T. fructose
1 egg   ½ tsp. salt
⅛ tsp. soda   3½ cups flour

Dissolve yeast in warm water. Add remaining ingredients. Mix
well. Roll into 12x24 rectangle. Spread with softened butter.
Sprinkle with desired amount of fructose and cinnamon. Fold in
half, cut in 1" strips and twist each strip. Let raise. **Bake at 350
degrees 15 minutes.**
Note: If using sugar to replace fructose, use 3 T.

HUSH PUPPIES

1 cup flour   ¾ cup cream-style corn
1 cup cornmeal   ½ cup chopped onion
2 tsp. baking powder   1 egg, beaten
½ tsp. salt   2 T. oil

Combine flour, cornmeal, baking powder and salt. Add corn,
onion, egg and oil; stir well. Drop batter into hot oil (370 degrees). Turn once. Drain on paper towels.

WHOLE WHEAT PIZZA CRUST

1 T. yeast   ½ tsp. salt
½ tsp. honey   1¾ cups water
½ cup warm water   1 T. oil
5 cups whole wheat flour

Dissolve yeast and honey in warm water. Let stand 10 minutes.
Stir in 4 cups flour, salt, water and oil. Mix well. Sprinkle remaining flour on board and knead 10 minutes. Let rise until
double.

CROISSANTS

1 cup warm water
1 T. yeast
¾ cup evaporated milk
2 T. honey
2 eggs
1 T. cold water

1½ tsp. salt
5½ cups flour
¼ cup butter, melted & cooled
1 cup cold butter, cut in ¼"
slices

Combine water and yeast until dissolved. Add milk, honey, 1 egg, salt and 1 cup flour. Beat until smooth. Blend in melted butter. Measure 3 cups flour and cold butter in another bowl. Mix until crumbly. Stir in remaining 1½ cup flour. Pour yeast mixture over flour mixture and stir until all moistened. Cover tightly and refrigerate until thoroughly chilled, at least 4 hours. Turn dough onto lightly floured surface. Knead 6 times. Divide into 4 equal parts. Shape 1 part at a time, leaving rest in refrigerator. Roll each part into 16" circle. Cut into 8 equal pie shaped wedges. Roll each wedge starting at wide edge and rolling to point. Place on ungreased cookie sheet 1½" apart. Curve ends to form crescent. Cover with plastic wrap. Let rise until double. Beat remaining egg and cold water. Brush over each roll. **Bake at 325 degrees 20-25 minutes.**

God loaned me a life and I must pay Him
back a portion of each day in loving service;
I must give a part of every hour I live in
thoughtful, kindly deeds to others who are
my sisters and my brothers

HONEY GLAZED ORANGE COFFEE CAKE

1 T. yeast
¼ cup warm water
½ cup warm milk
½ cup orange juice
¼ cup fructose

½ cup dairy sour cream
½ tsp. salt
4 cups flour
1 egg, lightly beaten

Dissolve yeast in warm water. Let stand 5-10 minutes. Stir in milk, fructose, sour cream, orange juice, salt and egg. Add flour and knead 5-8 minutes. Place in greased bowl and let rise until double. Grease 10" round pan. Divide dough into 3. Roll each portion into 20" long rope and braid all together. Coil into pan and let rise about 30 minutes. **Bake in 375 degree oven 25-30 minutes.** As soon as its out of oven glaze with ¼ cup honey and 2 T. butter melted together
Note: If using sugar to replace fructose, use ½ cup and for glaze use, 1 cup powdered sugar and 1-2 T. orange juice.

QUICK BISCUITS

2 cups self-rising flour

1 cup heavy cream

Combine and knead 5 minutes. Roll dough to ½" thickness. Cut with desired cutter. Place on greased cookie sheets. **Bake at 400 degrees 8-10 minutes.**

BEST EVER BISCUITS

2 cups flour
1 tsp. honey
½ tsp. salt
²/₃ cup milk

1 tsp. baking powder
½ tsp. cream of tartar
½ cup shortening

Combine all ingredients and **bake at 350 degrees 10-15 minutes.**

ANGEL BISCUITS

5 cups flour	2 T. honey
1 tsp. salt	1 tsp. baking powder
1 tsp. soda	1 cup shortening

Sift together dry ingredients and cut in shortening. Add 2 T. yeast dissolved in ¼ cup warm water. Warm and add 2 cups buttermilk. Mix until all flour is moistened. Roll out on floured board about 1" thick. Cut out with cookie cutter. Let raise 1½ hours. **Bake at 350 degrees 15-20 minutes.**
Variation: Mix in 1 cup raisins before buttermilk. Add 1¼ tsp cinnamon at last and mix just a little. Can frost if desired.

SOURDOUGH BISCUITS

1 T. yeast	⅛ cup fructose
1 cup warm water	4 tsp. baking powder
2 cups buttermilk	2 tsp. salt
¾ cup canola oil	¼ tsp. soda
6 cups or more flour	

Dissolve yeast in warm water. Combine all ingredients. Roll out, cut and **bake at 350 degrees 15-20 minutes.**
Note: If using sugar to replace fructose, use ¼ cup.

BAKING POWDER BISCUITS

1 cup whole wheat flour	1 tsp. salt
1 cup white flour	6 T. shortening
2 T. baking powder	⅔ cup milk

Sift all dry ingredients together. Cut in shortening. Mix in just enough milk to make soft dough, not too wet. Turn on floured board. Roll to ½" thickness. Cut with desired cutter. **Bake on greased cookie sheets at 375 degrees 15-20 minutes.**

BUTTERMILK BISCUITS

2 cups flour
1 T. baking powder
¾ tsp. salt

5 T. butter
1 cup buttermilk
½ tsp. soda

Sift together flour, baking powder, salt and soda. Cut in butter. Mix well. Add buttermilk. Roll dough to ¾". Cut with desired cutter. Place on ungreased sheet and **bake at 400 degrees 12-15 minutes.**

SWEET POTATO BISCUITS

2 cups flour
⅓ cup fructose
½ cup lard
½ cup milk

1 tsp. salt
3 tsp. baking powder
2 cups cooked, mashed
    sweet potatoes

Mix dry ingredients. Cut in lard. Add sweet potatoes and milk. Knead lightly. Roll, cut out and **bake at 375 degrees 15-20 minutes.**
Note: If using sugar to replace fructose, use ⅔ cup.

CHEESE BISCUITS

1 ⅔ cup flour
2 tsp. baking powder
½ tsp. salt
¼ tsp. soda

1 cup shredded cheddar
    cheese
¾ cup buttermilk
¼ cup shortening

Combine dry ingredients. Cut in shortening. Stir in cheese. Add buttermilk. Mix and knead slightly. Roll into 12" circle. Cut into 8 wedges. Begin at wide end of wedge and roll toward point. Place biscuit point side down on greased baking sheet. **Bake at 400 degrees 12-14 minutes.**

14

GARLIC-CHEESE BISCUITS

2 cups baking mix   ½ cup butter
⅔ cup water   ¼ tsp. garlic powder
½ cup shredded cheddar cheese

Combine baking mix, water and cheese until soft dough forms. Beat 30 seconds. Drop onto ungreased sheet. **Bake at 400 degrees 10-15 minutes.** Brush with melted butter and garlic powder. **Bake 1 more minute.**

WHOLE WHEAT MUFFINS

2 cups whole wheat flour   ½ tsp. soda
½ tsp. salt   1½ T. fructose
1 cup sour cream (may add a little more if needed)

Mix dry ingredients and add sour cream. Stir only until moistened. Fill 12 greased muffin tins ⅔ full. **Bake at 400 degrees 20-25 minutes.**
Note: If using sugar to replace fructose, use 3 T.

OATMEAL MUFFINS

1 cup oatmeal   ⅓ cup melted butter
1 cup buttermilk   ¾ cup flour
1 egg   ½ tsp. salt
¼ cup fructose   1 tsp. baking powder
1 T. molasses   ½ tsp. soda

Soak oatmeal in buttermilk 30 minutes. Add fructose, egg and molasses. Add butter and dry ingredients. Mix only until moistened. Fill greased muffin cups ⅔ full. **Bake at 375 degrees 20-25 minutes.** Makes 12.
Note: If using sugar to replace fructose, use ½ cup and increase flour to 1 cup.

BRAN MUFFINS

2 cups all bran
1 cup boiling water
½ cup butter or oleo
¼ cup honey
2 eggs
1 cup raisins

2 cups buttermilk
2½ cups flour
2½ tsp. soda
½ tsp. salt
1 cup dry all bran

Place 2 cups all bran in large bowl; add water and cool. Cream butter, honey and eggs. Add buttermilk and bran mixture. Combine flour, soda and salt and add to creamed mixture until moistened. Fold in raisins and dry all bran. Fill greased muffin tins ¾ full. **Bake at 350 degrees 20-25 minutes.**

APPLE MUFFINS

2 cups flour
1 tsp. soda
¼ tsp. cinnamon
¼ tsp. ginger
¼ tsp. salt
2 large eggs

1 cup plus 2 T. frozen
      apple juice
⅔ cup buttermilk
2 small peeled, chopped
      apples
⅓ cup chopped walnuts

Mix together flour, soda, cinnamon, ginger and salt. Mix together eggs, apple juice and buttermilk. Mix all together and stir just until moistened. Do not overmix. Fold in apples and nuts. Pour into greased muffin tins ⅔ full. **Bake at 350 degrees 20-25 minutes.**

If you walk with the Lord, you'll never be out of step.

MOLASSES APPLE MUFFINS

1½ cups flour
⅛ cup fructose
1 T. baking powder
1 tsp. cinnamon
¼ tsp. salt

1 peeled apple, finely cut
½ cup milk
¼ cup molasses
¼ cup oil
1 egg

Combine flour, fructose, baking powder, cinnamon and salt. Add apple and stir. Beat together milk, molasses, oil and egg. Stir into dry ingredients and mix just until blended. Fill 8 greased muffin cups. **Bake at 400 degrees 5 minutes. Reduce heat to 350 and bake 12-15 minutes.**
Note: If using sugar to replace fructose, use ¼ cup and increase flour to 2 cups.

BLUEBERRY MUFFINS

2 cups flour
3 tsp. baking powder
1 T. fructose
1 tsp. salt

1 egg
1 cup milk
¼ cup oil
1 cup fresh blueberries

Combine dry ingredients. Combine egg, milk and oil and pour into flour mixture. Stir just until moistened. Fold in blueberries. **Bake at 400 degrees 20 minutes or until done.**
Note: If using sugar to replace fructose, use 3 T.

God never shuts a door but He opens a window.

CREAM CHEESE BLUEBERRY MUFFINS

1½ cups flour
½ cup fructose
1½ tsp. baking powder
1 tsp. salt
½ tsp. soda

¾ cup orange juice
2 T. oil
1 egg
1 cup blueberries
1 (8oz.) cream cheese

Combine first 8 ingredients. Stir only until moistened. Fold in blueberries. Fill muffin cups ½ full. Cut cream cheese into 12 pieces. Push 1 cube into each muffin cup; cover with remaining batter. **Bake at 400 degrees 15-20 minutes.**
Note: If using sugar to replace fructose, use 1 cup and increase flour to 2 cups. May make without cream cheese if desired.

PINEAPPLE MUFFINS

2 cups flour
½ tsp. salt
¼ cup butter
1 cup unsweetened crushed pineapple, undrained

3 tsp. baking powder
⅛ cup honey
1 egg

Cream butter and honey and add dry ingredients. Add pineapple and stir just until moistened. Fill greased muffin tins ⅔ full. **Bake at 400 degrees 15-20 minutes.** Makes 12.

PUMPKIN MUFFINS

4 eggs
1 cup fructose
1 can (16oz.) pumpkin
1½ cups oil
2 cups unsweetened carob chips

2 tsp. soda
2 tsp. baking powder
1 tsp. cinnamon
1 tsp. salt
2¾ cups flour

Combine eggs, fructose and oil. Beat well. Combine dry ingredients and add to creamed mixture. Fold in chips. Fill 24 paper-lined muffin tins. **Bake at 400 degrees 15 minutes.**

ZUCCHINI MUFFINS

2 cups flour	¾ cup milk
1 T. baking powder	⅓ cup oil
1 tsp. cinnamon	¼ cup honey
½ tsp. salt	1 cup grated zucchini
2 eggs	½-1 cup raisins

Combine all ingredients just until moistened. Fill muffin cups (18 greased). **Bake at 350 degrees 20-25 minutes.**

MAPLE MUFFINS

2 cups flour	¼ cup maple syrup
2 tsp. baking powder	1½ cups sour cream
1¼ tsp. soda	1 egg
½ cup butter	½ cup chopped pecans

Preheat oven to 400 degrees. Grease 12 muffin tins. Mix together flour, baking powder, soda and salt. Beat butter until fluffy. Beat in maple syrup, sour cream and egg until blended. Add dry ingredients ½ cup at a time just until moistened. Stir in nuts. Spoon into muffin tins and **bake 15-20 minutes.**

ENGLISH MUFFINS

1½ cups milk   ¼ cup butter
Heat in pan until warm (130 degrees).
Combine: 2 T. honey   1 tsp. salt
                    1 T. yeast   1½ cups flour

Add liquids and beat 2 minutes. Beat in 1 egg and 1 cup flour. Add 2 more cups flour. Knead and let rise until doubled. Punch down and let rest 15 minutes. Roll dough ⅜" thick and cut in 3" circles. Dip both sides in cornmeal and place on cookie sheets. Cover and let rise until double. **Fry in oiled skillet on medium heat 8 minutes on each side.** Makes 18 muffins.

PUMPKIN BUNS

2 T. yeast
¼ cup honey
½ cup warm milk
2 cups flour
1 cup yellow cornmeal

1 tsp. salt
1 cup buttermilk
½ cup pumpkin
½ cup butter, softened
1 egg

Dissolve yeast in warm milk. Let stand 10 minutes. Mix together dry ingredients. Beat together buttermilk, pumpkin, butter, honey and egg. Stir into yeast mixture. Beat dry ingredients in ½ cup at a time until blended. Cover loosely and let rise until doubled. Fill 12 greased muffin tins and let rise again 30 minutes. **Bake at 350 degrees 15-20 minutes.**

SWEET POTATO DINNER ROLLS

½ cup warm water
²/₃ cup honey
2 eggs, beaten
7 cups flour
²/₃ cup cooked, mashed sweet potatoes

½ cup oil
1½ tsp. salt
1 cup scalded, cooled milk
2 T. yeast

Dissolve yeast in warm water. Add honey, eggs, oil, sweet potatoes, salt and milk. Add flour. Knead 5 minutes. Let raise until double. Roll out on floured board. Cut with round cookie cutter. Let raise until double. **Bake at 350 degrees for 15-20 minutes.** Makes good hamburger buns.

The man who walks with God always gets to his destination

20

CINNAMON ROLLS

2 T. yeast
1 cup water (warm)
1 cup milk (scalded and cooled)
1/3 cup fructose

2 eggs
1/2 tsp. salt
1/2 cup soft butter
6-7 cups flour

Dissolve yeast in water. Blend all together. Let raise. Roll out into rectangle. Spread with soft butter, fructose and cinnamon. Roll into jelly roll, slice and let raise. **Bake at 350 degrees 15 minutes.**

ONION DINNER ROLLS

3/4 cup milk
3/4 cup onion, chop fine
1/4 cup honey
3 T. butter

1 1/2 tsp. salt
1 T. yeast
1/2 cup warm water
4-5 cups flour

Combine milk, onion, honey, butter and salt. Bring to simmer and cook 5 minutes. Cool. Dissolve yeast in warm water. Add cooled milk mixture to yeast; mix well. Stir in flour. Knead 5-10 minutes. Let rise until doubled. Divide dough in 12 pieces. Roll each in a ball and flatten slightly. Place 2" apart in greased 9"x13" pan. Let rise until doubled. Brush rolls with lightly beaten egg. **Bake at 350 degrees 20-30 minutes.**

GLAZE FOR ROLLS

1/2 cup fructose
1 T. molasses
1/4 cup butter

1 1/2 tsp. white vinegar
1/2 tsp. vanilla
2 T. corn syrup

Mix all together in saucepan. Bring to a boil over medium heat. Boil 1 minute. Remove from heat.
Note: If using sugar to replace fructose, use 1 cup packed brown sugar and omit molasses.

HOMEMADE BREAD

5 cups warm water
¾ cup oil
1 T. salt
4-5 cups whole wheat flour

3 T. yeast
¾ cup honey
2 T. vinegar
8-10 cups white flour

Mix all together and knead 8-10 minutes. Let rise until doubled. Make into 6 loaves and let rise again. **Bake at 350 degrees 30 minutes.**

WHITE BREAD I

2 T. yeast
½ cup honey
11 cups flour
¼ cup oil

1 T. salt
½ cup warm water
3 cups warm water

Dissolve yeast in ½ cup water. Add remaining ingredients and knead 5-10 minutes. Let rise until double. Divide in 4 and let rest 10 minutes. Shape into 4 loaves and let rise. **Bake at 350 degrees 25-35 minutes.**

WHITE BREAD II

3 T. yeast
3½ cups warm water
¾ cup oil
¼ cup honey

½ cup dry milk
1- 2 T. salt
10 cups bread flour

Dissolve yeast in water. Add oil. Mix in honey. Mix ½ of flour with dry milk and salt. Mix well with liquid. Add rest of flour. Knead 10 minutes. Let rise until double. Divide into 1½ lb. loaves and let rest 10 minutes. Shape into loaves. Let rise. **Bake at 350 degrees 25-30 minutes.**

22

WHITE BREAD III

1½ qts. warm water   1¼ T. salt
5 T. melted butter   1 cup honey
¼ cup yeast   12 cups flour

Dissolve yeast in warm water. Add remaining ingredients. Knead 5-10 minutes. Let rise until doubled. Put in greased bread pans and let rise again. **Bake at 350 degrees 30 minutes.** Makes 4 loaves.

HONEY WHOLE WHEAT BREAD

3 cups whole wheat flour   3 cups water
½ cup dry milk   ½ cup honey
1 T. salt   2 T. oil
2 T. yeast   5-5½ cups flour

Heat water, honey and oil until warm. Mix yeast, dry milk and salt. Pour warm liquids over yeast mixture and mix well. Add flour and knead 5 minutes. Put in greased bowl and let rise until double. Divide in half and let rest 10 minutes. Shape into 2 loaves. Put into greased bread pans. Let rise. **Bake at 350 degrees 25-35 minutes.**

Patience is the ability to put up with people
you'd like to put down,

OATMEAL BREAD

2 cups quick oats
1 cup white flour
¾ cup honey
2 T. salt
4 T. butter or oleo

4 cups boiling water
2 T. yeast
1 cup warm water
10½-11 cups flour

Combine first 5 ingredients. Pour over this boiling water. Stir well and let cool to lukewarm. Mix yeast and warm water. Let set to dissolve. Add to first mixture. Stir in flour. Knead 5-10 minutes. Place in greased bowl. Cover and let rise until double. Punch down and let raise again. Divide into 4 pieces. Let rest 10 minutes. Shape into loaves and put into loaf pans. Let rise until just over the top of pan. **Bake at 350 degrees 25-30 minutes.**

RYE BREAD

1 T. yeast
1 cup warm water
1 cup milk, scalded, cooled
1 T. salt

2 T. oil
2 T. molasses
2 cups rye flour
4½ cups white flour

Dissolve yeast in water. Add remaining ingredients and mix well. Knead 5-10 minutes. Let rise until double. Divide in half and let rest 10 minutes. Shape into 2 loaves. Put in greased bread pans. Let rise. **Bake at 350 degrees 25-35 minutes.**

People who start the day on their knees
generally go through it on their toes.

CORN BREAD I

¾ lb. sweet potatoes, cooked,
            mashed
¾ cup yellow cornmeal
2 T. flour
1 T. baking powder
¾ tsp. salt

½ tsp. soda
⅛ tsp. pepper
1 egg, lightly beaten
¾ cup buttermilk
3 T. butter, melted

Preheat oven to 375 degrees. Sift together dry ingredients. Add egg and buttermilk to sweet potatoes and mix well. Add butter and dry ingredients and stir just until blended. Pour batter into greased 9"x9" pan. **Bake 20-25 minutes.**

CORN BREAD II

2 cups cornmeal
½ cup white or wheat flour
½ tsp. soda
1 T. honey

1 egg white
1 T. oil
2 cups plain yogurt

Stir together dry ingredients. Combine wet ingredients. Combine both and gently stir. Stir only until moistened. **Bake at 400 degrees in oiled 8"x8" pan 20-25 minutes.**

CORN BREAD III

1 cup flour
3 tsp. baking powder
½ tsp. salt
1 cup cornmeal

1 cup milk
2 eggs, beaten
¼ cup honey
¼ cup oil

Add liquids to dry ingredients. Stir just until moist. **Bake in greased 8"x8" pan at 375 degrees 20 minutes.**

MEXICAN CORN BREAD

1½ cups yellow corn meal
3 tsp. baking powder
¾ tsp. salt
1 T. honey
3 eggs
1 cup sour cream

1 cup grated cheese
1 (8½ oz.) corn
⅓ cup jalapeno peppers,
　　　　　　opt.
⅓ cup oil
½ cup onion, chopped

Mix dry ingredients well. Add remaining ingredients and mix. Add milk if too thick. Pour into greased 9"x13" pan. **Bake at 400 degrees 15-20 minutes.**

PUMPKIN CORN BREAD

1 cup flour
1 cup cornmeal
¼ cup honey
2 tsp. baking powder
½ tsp. salt

1 cup cooked, mashed
　　　　　pumpkin
¼ cup butter, melted
2 eggs

Combine dry ingredients and mix well. Add combined remaining ingredients and beat 1 minute. Spread into greased 8"x8" pan. **Bake at 400 degrees 20-25 minutes.**

GARLIC BREAD

1 stick butter or oleo
¼ cup salad dressing
¼ tsp. paprika

⅓ cup parmesan cheese
½ tsp. garlic powder

Mix all together and spread generously on french bread. **Put under broiler and broil until golden brown.**

26

CHEESE BREAD

2 T. yeast
²/₃ cup warm water
2½ cups warm water
5 cups bread flour

2 cups whole wheat flour
2 tsp. salt
2 cups shredded cheddar
          cheese

Dissolve yeast in ²/₃ cup water. Mix together both flours, salt and cheese. Add 2½ cups water to yeast mixture. Beat all together. Knead 5-10 minutes. Add more flour if needed. Let rise until doubled. Shape into 2 loaves and put in greased loaf pans. Let rise 20 minutes. **Bake at 350 degrees 25-30 minutes.**

GINGERBREAD

1 cup molasses
½ cup lard
1 cup buttermilk
4 cups flour

1 egg
1 tsp. soda
¼ tsp. salt
1 T. ginger

Beat together molasses, lard, buttermilk and 2 cups flour. Add egg. Mix remaining dry ingredients together and add to mixture. Pour into greased 9"x13" pan. **Bake at 350 degrees 20-30 minutes.**

True Joy comes from putting
Jesus first
Others second
Yourself last

27

APPLE GINGERBREAD

½ cup whole bran cereal
½ cup molasses
¼ cup butter, soft
¼ cup boiling water
1 egg
1 cup flour
½ tsp. soda
¼ tsp. salt

½ tsp. baking powder
½ tsp. ginger
6 cups sliced, peeled
    apples
¼ cup melted butter
¼ cup white syrup
milk

Mix bran, molasses, butter and water. Add egg and beat; let stand 5 minutes. Mix together dry ingredients and add to first mixture and stir only until blended. Pour into greased 8"x8" pan. **Bake in 350 degree oven 20 minutes.** Arrange apples in layers over top. Brush with mixture of butter and syrup. **Bake 10 more minutes.** Remove from oven and brush with milk. Broil until apples brown.

PUMPKIN BREAD I

⅓ cup softened butter
2 T. honey
2 eggs
1 cup pumpkin
1½ cups flour
1 tsp. baking powder
1 tsp. soda

1½ tsp. cinnamon
1 tsp. ginger
¼ tsp. salt
¼ tsp. nutmeg
½ cup buttermilk
1 cup quick oatmeal
½ cup chopped dates

Cream together butter, honey and eggs. Add pumpkin and mix well. Combine dry ingredients and add alternately with buttermilk to creamed mixture. Fold in oatmeal and dates. Pour into greased loaf pan and **bake at 350 degrees for 40-45 minutes.**

PUMPKIN BREAD II

¾ cup fructose
1⅓ cups flour
¼ tsp. baking powder
1 tsp. soda
¾ tsp. salt
½ cup nuts (opt.)

½ tsp. cinnamon
½ cup oil
½ cup frozen apple juice,
                thawed
1 cup pumpkin
2 eggs

Combine fructose, flour, baking powder, soda, salt, cinnamon, oil, apple juice, pumpkin and eggs. Fold in nuts. Spread in well greased loaf pan. **Bake at 350 degrees 1 hour or until done.** Note: If using sugar to replace fructose, use 1½ cups and increase flour ⅓ cup.

BUTTERNUT SQUASH BREAD

2 T. yeast
½ cup warm water
1 cup warm milk
1 T. salt
1¼ cups cooked, mashed squash

2 eggs, beaten
⅓ cup melted butter
⅓ cup honey
7½ cups flour

Dissolve yeast in warm water. Add rest of ingredients and knead 5-8 minutes. Let rise until doubled. Punch down dough. Shape into 3 loaves and put into 3 greased bread pans. Let rise one half hour. **Bake at 350 degrees 25-30 minutes.**

What sort of church would our church be if
every member were just like me?

ZUCCHINI BREAD

2½ cups flour
1 tsp. salt
1 tsp. soda
1 tsp. baking powder
1 cup fructose
2 tsp. vanilla
3 eggs

1 cup butter
1 cup drained, crushed
pineapple
2 cups grated zucchini
½ cup nuts (opt.)
½ cup raisins (opt.)

Mix fructose, butter, eggs and vanilla. Add pineapple and zucchini. Mix in flour, soda, baking powder, salt, nuts and raisins. Pour into 2 greased loaf pans. **Bake at 350 degrees 45-50 minutes.**
Note: If using sugar to replace fructose, use 2 cups and add ½ cup more flour.

CINNAMON BREAD

2 cups milk
2 T. fructose or honey
¼ cup butter
1¼ tsp. salt

2 T. yeast
¼ cup warm water
6 cups flour

Heat milk. Combine fructose, butter and salt. Add hot milk and cool to lukewarm. Dissolve yeast in warm water and let stand 5-10 minutes. Add to cooled milk mixture. Stir in flour 1 cup at a time. Knead until smooth 5-10 minutes. Let rise until doubled. Punch down dough and divide in half. Roll each into 13"x9" rectangle. Spread evenly with softened butter. Sprinkle with desired amount of fructose and cinnamon. Sprinkle with raisins if desired. Starting at short end roll up as a jelly roll. Place loaves into greased bread pans. Let rise until double. **Bake at 350 degrees 25-30 minutes.** Makes 2 loaves.
Note: If using sugar to replace fructose use 4 T.

SUNFLOWER BREAD

1 T. yeast
1½ tsp. salt
3-3½ cups flour
3 T. oil
1 cup warm water

1 cup toasted sunflower
seeds
¼ cup honey
1 cup wheat bran

Dissolve yeast and honey in warm water. Add wheat bran, oil and salt. Stir in flour. Knead 5-10 minutes. Let rise until double. Sprinkle on sunflower seeds and knead 5 minutes. Shape into loaf and put into greased loaf pan. **Bake at 350 degrees 30-35 minutes.**

ENGLISH MUFFIN BREAD

5½-6 cups flour
2 T. yeast
½ T. honey
2 tsp. salt

¼ tsp. soda
2 cups milk, scalded and
cooled
½ cup water

Combine cooled milk, yeast (dissolved in water), honey, salt and soda. Add 3½ cups flour. Then add enough flour to make stiff dough. Spoon into 2 greased loaf pans that have been sprinkled with cornmeal. Top with cornmeal. Cover and let rise 45 minutes. **Bake at 350 degrees 25-30 minutes.**

The best thing parents can do for their
children is to love each other.

31

FRENCH BREAD

1 T. fructose
2 scant T. salt
2 T. lard or oil
2 cups boiling water

2 T. yeast
½ cup warm water
½ T. honey
6 cups flour

Combine first 4 ingredients and cool. Combine next 3 ingredients and dissolve. Combine both together and work in flour with a spoon. Work down every 10 minutes 4-5 times. Divide into 2 balls; let rest 10 minutes. Roll out less than ½" thick. Roll up as jelly roll; place on greased cookie sheet. Let rise until double. Slash several times. Brush with 1 beaten egg and 2 T. milk. Sprinkle with sesame seeds. **Bake at 350 degrees 25 minutes.**
Note: If using sugar to replace fructose, use 2 T.

STREUSEL TOPPING FOR COFFEE CAKES

$\frac{1}{8}$ cup fructose
2 T. butter

2 T. biscuit mix
2 tsp. cinnamon

Mix all together and put on coffee cake.
Note: If using sugar to replace fructose, use ¼ cup.

Desserts

Notes

APRICOT COBBLER

Filling:
¼ cup fructose	2 T. cornstarch
1 T. butter	½ tsp. cinnamon

2- 1 lb. cans unsweetened apricots, drained, save juice
Topping:
½ cup flour	¼ tsp. salt
¼ cup fructose	2 T. softened butter
¾ tsp. baking powder	1 egg

In saucepan mix fructose and cornstarch. Stir in 1 cup reserved juice. Cook over medium heat until thickened. Stir in butter and cinnamon. Spoon into 1½ qt. casserole. For topping, mix together flour, fructose, baking powder, salt, butter and egg. Spoon over fruit. **Bake at 350 30-35 minutes.** Serve warm with ice cream.
Note: If using sugar to replace fructose, use ½ cup in each.

BLUEBERRY COBBLER

3 cups fresh or frozen blueberries	1 cup water
2½ T. cornstarch, dissolved in a little water	½ cup fructose

Combine all ingredients and cook until thick. Pour into 1½ qt. casserole.
Topping:
½ cup flour	¼ tsp. salt
¼ cup fructose	2 T. butter, softened
¾ tsp. baking powder	1 egg

Combine all together and spoon on top of fruit. **Bake at 350 degrees 25-30 minutes.**
Note: If using sugar to replace fructose, use ¾ cup in fruit and ½ cup in topping.

FRESH BERRY CRISP

Crust and crumb topping:

½ cup ground almonds	1 cup flour
¼ cup fructose	½ cup less 1 T. butter

Filling:

¼ cup fructose	1½ T. flour

2 pints fresh berries, blueberries, strawberries or raspberries

Combine crust ingredients until coarse crumbs form. Press half of crumbs in 9" square baking pan. Combine filling ingredients and spoon on top of crust. Sprinkle remaining crumbs on top. **Bake at 350 degrees 35-40 minutes.**
Note: If using sugar to replace fructose, use ½ cup in crumbs and ½ cup in filling.

FRUIT CRUMBLE

2½ cups fruit of your choice
Place in greased 8"x8" pan.
Combine until crumbly:

1 cup flour	dash of salt
1 egg	¼ cup fructose
½ tsp. cinnamon	1 tsp. baking powder

Sprinkle over fruit and drizzle ¼ cup melted butter over all. **Bake at 375 degrees 25 minutes.**
Note: If using sugar to replace fructose, use ½ cup.

The Lord wants our precious time, not our spare time.

PUMPKIN CUSTARD

1½ cups pumpkin
¾ cup fructose
2 T. flour, rounded
½ tsp. cinnamon
4 eggs

½ tsp. nutmeg
1 tsp. vanilla
½ tsp. lemon juice
4 cups milk
½ tsp. salt

Mix all and pour into large casserole. **Bake at 350 degrees until done.**
Note: If using sugar to replace fructose, use 1½ cups.

BREAD PUDDING

2 cups bread crumbs
¼ cup fructose
dash of salt
½ tsp. vanilla

4 eggs, beaten
2 cups milk
½ tsp. cinnamon

Put crumbs in baking pan. Mix remaining ingredients and pour over crumbs. Add raisins if desired and dot with butter. **Bake at 350 degrees until set.** Serve warm.
Note: If using sugar to replace fructose, use ½ cup.

LEMON PUDDING

½ cup less 1 T. fructose
¼ tsp. salt
1 T. butter
2 egg yolks, beaten

3 T. cornstarch
¾ cup water
½ cup lemon juice

Mix fructose, salt and cornstarch in saucepan. Gradually stir in water. Boil over direct heat, stirring constantly. Boil 1 minute. Remove from heat. Stir ½ of hot mixture into egg yolks. Blend into remaining mixture. Boil 1 minute. Remove from heat. Add butter and lemon juice.

CHOCOLATE OR CAROB PUDDING

2 egg whites
$^2/_3$ cup cocoa or carob powder
2 T. cornstarch
2¼ cups milk, divided

¼ cup fructose
$^1/_8$ tsp. salt
1 tsp. vanilla

Lightly beat egg whites and set aside. Combine cocoa and corn-starch. Stir in ¾ cup milk and beat until smooth. In saucepan combine remaining milk, fructose and salt. Mix well. Bring to boil stirring constantly. Remove from heat. Stir cocoa mixture into hot milk mixture. Bring to boil and boil 2 minutes stirring constantly. Remove from heat. Gradually stir 1 cup hot cocoa mixture into egg whites. Cook over medium 2 minutes stirring constantly. Do not boil. Remove from heat; add vanilla.
Note: If using sugar to replace fructose, use ½ cup.

HOT FUDGE PUDDING

¾ cup flour
$^1/_3$ cup fructose
2 T. carob or cocoa powder
2 tsp. baking powder

¼ tsp. salt
½ cup milk
2 T. melted butter

Combine all ingredients and mix well. Pour into greased 2 qt. baking dish.

Topping:
$^1/_3$ cup fructose
$^1/_3$ cup carob or cocoa powder

2 T. molasses
2 cups boiling water

Combine all topping ingredients and gently pour over above cake. **Bake at 350 degrees 35-40 minutes.** Serve warm with ice cream.
Note: If using sugar to replace fructose, use ¾ cup in cake and ½ cup white and ½ cup brown in topping. Omit molasses and increase flour to 1 cup in cake.

PUMPKIN PUDDING

Crust:
1 cup flour
½ cup butter
Pudding:
4 cups pumpkin
1 cup fructose
4 eggs

1 cup unsweetened
    coconut

½ cup evaporated milk
1 tsp. vanilla
2 tsp. cinnamon

Mix crust ingredients and press into bottom of 9"x13" pan. **Bake at 350 degrees 10 minutes.** While crust is baking blend together pudding ingredients. Pour over crust and bake additional 30 minutes. Serve with whipped cream or ice cream.
Note: If using sugar to replace fructose, use 2 cups.

VANILLA PUDDING

Heat 3 cups milk. Add 4 beaten eggs, ½ cup fructose and 2 heaping T. cornstarch in a little milk. Cook until thick and smooth. Add vanilla and butter.
Note: If using sugar to replace fructose, use 1 cup.

RHUBARB TAPIOCA

1 cup baby pearl tapioca
5 cups rhubarb
1 lg. box sugar-free strawberry jello

2 qts. water
1 qt. water
1½ cups fructose

Cook tapioca in 2 qts. water until starts boiling, stirring occasionally. Turn off and let set on burner covered 30 minutes. Cook rhubarb with 1 qt. water until tender. Stir in jello and fructose. Mix with tapioca and chill.
Note: If using sugar to replace fructose, use 2½-3 cups.

FRUIT TAPIOCA

8 cups water
1 scant cup tapioca
¼ cup fructose
⅛ tsp. salt

2 sm. boxes sugar-free
    jello, any flavor
2-4 cups fruit
1 lg. lite cool whip

Boil water slowly and add tapioca. Simmer 20 minutes uncovered until nearly clear. Remove from heat. Add jello, salt and sweetener. Cover and let set 20 minutes and refrigerate. When set add fruit and cool whip. Can use whipped cream to replace cool whip.

FRUIT PIZZA

Crust:
2½ cups whole wheat flour   1 T. fructose
1 cup margarine or butter
Mix thoroughly. Press into pizza pan and **bake at 325 degrees 15 minutes.**

Cream filling:
1 pkg. cream cheese   3 T. fructose
1 cup whipped cream
Beat cream cheese and fructose together. Fold in whipped cream. Spread on cooled crust.

Fruit topping:
Assorted fruit (strawberries, grapes, blueberries, peaches, pineapple chunks, oranges, raspberries, etc.)
Arrange fruit in eye-pleasing design on top of cream filling.

Glaze:
¼ cup peach or pineapple juice   ½ cup orange juice
2 T. lemon juice   dash of salt
2 T. fructose   1 T. cornstarch
Bring to a boil in saucepan until thick. Spoon over fruit. Refrigerate 1 hour before serving.

DAIRY QUEEN

Soak 2 T. knox gelatin in ½ cup cold water. Heat 4 cups milk, hot but not boiling. Remove from heat. Add gelatin and 1 cup fructose, 2 tsp. vanilla and 1 scant tsp. salt. Cool and add 3 cups cream. Put in ice box and chill 5-6 hours before freezing. Makes 1 gallon.
Note: If using sugar to replace fructose, use 2 cups.

HONEY COCONUT ICE CREAM

1 cup honey
4 eggs, beaten
3 cups heavy cream
1 cup unsweetened coconut
½ tsp. lemon extract

½ tsp. salt
3 cups milk
2 tsp. vanilla
2 (8½oz.) cans unsweet-
ened crushed pineapple

Mix all together and put in gallon freezer and freeze.

STRAWBERRY ICE CREAM

8 T. flour
1½ cups fructose
½ tsp. salt

5 cups milk
4 eggs, beaten
1-2 T. vanilla

Combine flour and fructose. Gradually add milk and eggs. Cook over medium heat until thick. Add vanilla. Cover and let cool in refrigerator 2 hours. When cool add:
1½ cups fresh strawberries,
              blended
2 tsp. lemon juice

4 cups cream, can use
         half milk

Put in gallon freezer and freeze.
Note: If using sugar to replace fructose, use 2-2½ cups.

BUTTERSCOTCH SAUCE

¾ cup fructose
¼ cup butter
¾ cup evaporated milk

2 T. molasses
⅔ cup light corn syrup

Combine fructose, butter, corn syrup and molasses in heavy saucepan over medium heat; stir until butter melts and ingredients are blended. Bring to a boil; cook to soft-ball stage, or 235 degrees on candy thermometer. Remove from heat, cool slightly. Add milk slowly, stirring until blended. Store in refrigerator. Serve over ice cream.
Note: If using sugar to replace fructose, use 1½ cups brown sugar and omit molasses.

BUTTERSCOTCH TOPPING

½ cup fructose
1½ T. molasses
¼ cup rich milk

2 T. white syrup
3 T. butter

Combine all ingredients. Bring to boil and simmer 3 minutes.
Note: If using sugar to replace fructose, use 1 cup brown sugar and omit molasses.

CARAMEL SAUCE

½ cup fructose
2 T. molasses
4 T. flour

3 cups boiling water
¼ lb. butter
1½ tsp. vanilla

Mix flour, fructose and molasses. Add water a little at a time. Bring to a boil, cover and simmer 5 minutes. Remove from heat; add butter and vanilla.
Note: If using sugar to replace fructose, use ½ cup brown, ¼ cup white and omit molasses.

42

CHOCOLATE SAUCE

3 (1oz.) squares unsweetened
                 chocolate
½ cup fructose
¼ tsp. salt
1 tsp. vanilla

1¾ cups cream
¼ cup flour
1 T. butter
½ cup slivered almonds,
                opt.

Melt chocolate in cream in double boiler over hot water. Cook until smooth, stirring occasionally. Combine fructose, flour and salt. Add enough chocolate mixture to make smooth paste. Add to remaining chocolate mixture. Cook until smooth and thick. Add butter, vanilla and almonds; blend well. Serve over ice cream.
Note: If using sugar to replace fructose, use 1 cup.

HOT FUDGE SAUCE I

1 stick butter
½ tsp. salt
1½ cups evaporated milk

1½ cups fructose
3 squares unsweetened
                chocolate

Melt butter and chocolate in double boiler. Stir in fructose, salt and milk gradually. Return to heat and cook a few minutes.
Note: If using sugar to replace fructose, use 3 cups.

HOT FUDGE SAUCE II

½ cup butter
2 squares chocolate
1½ cups fructose

½ tsp. salt
1 lg. can evaporated milk
1 tsp. vanilla

Melt butter in double boiler. Add chocolate and melt. Slowly add fructose and salt. Add milk and cook until fructose is dissolved. Add vanilla. Cool and store in refrigerator. Heat before serving.
Note: If using sugar to replace fructose, use 3 cups.

OLD-FASHIONED HERSHEYS SYRUP

1 cup Hersheys cocoa
dash of salt
¼ cup fructose

1 cup hot water
2 tsp. vanilla

Mix fructose, salt and cocoa with ⅓ cup hot water. Add rest of water, stirring. Boil 3 minutes. Makes 2 cups.

PIE CRUST I

3 cups flour
¾ cup shortening
1 egg

5 T. water
pinch of salt
1 T. vinegar

Mix flour and shortening. Beat egg and add vinegar, salt and water. Mix well and roll out.

PIE CRUST II

4 cups flour
2 tsp. salt

2 cups shortening

Mix thoroughly with pastry blender. Make a paste with 1 cup water and 1 cup flour and add to above mixture and toss lightly. Makes 10 pie crusts.

PIE CRUST III

3 cups flour
5 T. water
½ tsp. salt

1 cup lard
1 egg
1 T. vinegar

Cut lard into flour and salt mixture. Add rest of ingredients. Roll out as desired.

44

QUICK PIE CRUST

1½ cups flour   ½ cup oil
1 tsp. salt   2 T. milk

Mix all together. Pat out with fingers in a 9" pie plate. Add desired filling and bake.

GRAHAM CRACKER CRUST I

1½ cups graham cracker crumbs (about 18 single crackers)
1 T. fructose   ⅓ cup melted butter

Mix together thoroughly. Press into 9" pie plate. Chill as is or
bake at 350 degrees 8 minutes.
Note: If using sugar to replace fructose, use 2 T.

GRAHAM CRACKER CRUST II

1⅓ cups graham cracker crumbs   ¼ cup melted butter
⅛ cup fructose

Combine all together and press in pie pan. **Bake at 350 degrees 8-10 minutes.**
Note: If using sugar to replace fructose, use ¼ cup.

Peace is seeing a sunset and knowing who to thank.

APPLE PIE

5 cups chopped, peeled apples
$^1/_3$ cup fructose
2 T. flour
Topping:
$^1/_4$ cup fructose
$^1/_2$ cup butter

1 tsp. cinnamon
$^1/_2$ tsp. nutmeg
1 9" unbaked pie shell

$^1/_2$ cup flour

Combine apples, fructose, flour, cinnamon and nutmeg. Spoon into pie shell. Combine topping ingredients until coarse crumbs. Sprinkle over pie. **Bake at 400 degrees 10 minutes. Reduce heat to 350 and bake 40-45 minutes**
Note: If using sugar to replace fructose, use $^1/_2$ cup in pie and $^1/_2$ cup in topping.

APPLE CRUMB PIE

6 apples
$^1/_2$ cup fructose
$^1/_3$ cup butter

$^3/_4$ cup flour
1 tsp. cinnamon
1 9" pie shell

Pare apples and slice into unbaked pie shell. Mix $^1/_4$ cup fructose and cinnamon and sprinkle over apples. Combine remaining fructose and flour. Add butter and rub together to form crumbs. Sprinkle crumbs over apples. **Bake at 425 degrees 10 minutes. Reduce heat to 350 degrees and bake 35 minutes longer.**
Note: If using sugar to replace fructose, use 1 cup. Use half the sugar in the crumbs.

No matter how much we have failed, the love of God never ceases.

46

APPLE CREAM PIE

4 cups sliced, peeled apples   1 cup cream
½ cup fructose   1 9" unbaked pie shell
3 T. flour

Place apples in pie shell. Combine fructose, flour and cream. Pour over apples and sprinkle with cinnamon. **Bake at 400 degrees 10 minutes. Reduce heat to 350 and bake 35-40 minutes.**
Note: If using sugar to replace fructose, use ¾ cup.

APPLE RAISIN PIE

4½ cups peeled, sliced apples   ¼ tsp. salt
¼ cup raisins $^1/_8$ cup cream
$^1/_3$ cup maple syrup   ¾ tsp. cinnamon
¼ cup flour   1 double pie crust,unbaked

Combine all ingredients and put into pie crust. Put on top crust and brush with milk. **Bake at 350 degrees 45-50 minutes.**

BLUEBERRY PIE

4 cups blueberries   3 T. butter
1 cup water   ¼ tsp. salt
½ cup fructose   9" graham cracker crust
$^1/_3$ cup flour

Pour 3 cups blueberries into crust. Cook remaining cup of berries with water, fructose and flour until thickened. When thick, put into blender with butter and salt. Blend well. Pour over berries in crust. Refrigerate 5 hours or overnight. Serve with cool whip.
Note: If using sugar to replace fructose, use 1 cup.

FRESH PEACH PIE

Crush 3 ripe peaches and add:

3 T. cornstarch   ½ cup fructose
½ cup water   ¼ tsp. cinnamon

Cook on medium heat until thick and clear. Slice 4 peaches in 9" baked pie shell. Pour slightly cooled mixture over top. Top with whipped cream.
Note: If using sugar to replace fructose, use 1 cup.

FRESH STRAWBERRY PIE

1½ cups water   1 qt. strawberries, sliced
½ cup fructose   1 baked pie shell
2 T. cornstarch   whipped cream
1 (3oz.) pkg. sugar-free strawberry jello

Cook together water, fructose and cornstarch, stirring until clear and thick. Remove from heat and add jello. Cool 10 minutes in cold water. Place strawberries in pie shell. Pour jello mixture over strawberries and chill until set. Cover with whipped cream. Can use this same recipe using fresh peaches and sugar free peach jello.
Note: If using sugar to replace fructose, use ¾ cup.

STRAWBERRY PIE

1 pkg. sugar-free vanilla pudding (not instant)
1 pkg. sugar-free strawberry gelatin
2½ cups cold water   1 9" baked pie shell
4 cups strawberries   whipped cream

Mix pudding, gelatin and water. Stir over medium heat until mixture comes to a boil. Remove from heat; cool in refrigerator until slightly thick. Arrange strawberries in pie shell. Pour cooled mixture over berries. Chill until set. Serve with whipped cream.

PUMPKIN PIE

1 unbaked pie shell
2 eggs
½ cup fructose
2 T. molasses
2 T. flour
2 cups pumpkin

½ tsp. salt
½ tsp. ginger
¾ tsp. cinnamon
¼ cup evaporated milk
½ cup milk or cream

Blend all ingredients in blender and pour into pie shell. **Bake at 350 degrees 45-50 minutes.**
Note: If using sugar to replace fructose, use ½ cup white, ½ cup brown and omit molasses.

FROZEN PUMPKIN PIE

1 cup canned pumpkin
¼ cup fructose
1 qt. sugar-free vanilla ice cream

¼ tsp. nutmeg
½ tsp. ginger
½ tsp. salt

Mix pumpkin, fructose, salt, nutmeg and ginger. Add to softened ice cream and mix well. Pour into 10" baked graham cracker crust. Put ½ pecan on each piece for decoration if desired. Put in freezer. Best made the day before.
Note: If using sugar to replace fructose, use ½ cup.

RAISIN PIE

1 cup raisins
⅓ cup fructose
¾ cup water
¼ tsp. salt

½ cup milk
2 egg yolks, beaten
1 T. cornstarch
1 baked pie shell

Cook raisins, fructose, water and salt together. Mix egg yolks, cornstarch and milk and pour into raisins. Cook until thickened. Pour into baked pie shell. Top with meringue made with 2 stiffly beaten egg whites. **Brown in oven.**
Note: If using sugar to replace fructose, use ⅔ cup.

RHUBARB CUSTARD PIE

2 eggs
¾ cup fructose
½ tsp. nutmeg
2 tsp. butter

2 T. milk
3 T. flour
3 cups chopped rhubarb

Combine all ingredients but butter. Mix well. Pour into unbaked pie shell. Dot with butter. **Bake at 350 degrees 45-50 minutes.**
Note: If using sugar to replace fructose, use 1½ cups.

RHUBARB-RASPBERRY PIE

$^1/_3$ cup flour
1 cup fructose
1 cup raspberries
pastry for 2 crust 9" pie

1 T. lemon juice
3 cups chopped rhubarb
1½ T. butter

Preheat oven to 400 degrees. Mix together lemon juice, flour and fructose; pour over rhubarb and raspberries and toss to coat. Place in unbaked pie shell. Dot with butter. Cover with top crust. **Bake for 40-50 minutes.**
Note: If using sugar to replace fructose, use 2 cups.

SQUASH PIE

2 cups yellow squash
½ cup fructose
1 T. molasses
½ tsp. salt
$^1/_8$ tsp. ginger

½ tsp. cinnamon
$^1/_8$ tsp. nutmeg
2 eggs
½ cup milk
1 T. flour

Combine ingredients in blender and pour into unbaked pie shell. **Bake at 350 degrees 45-50 minutes.**
Note: If using sugar to replace fructose, use ½ cup white, ½ cup brown and omit molasses.

MAPLE-SQUASH PIE

2 cups cooked, mashed squash   ½ tsp. ginger
1 cup evaporated milk   3 eggs
¼ cup honey   1 unbaked pie shell
½ cup pure maple syrup   whipped cream
½ tsp. cinnamon

Mix ingredients well and pour into pie shell. **Bake at 350 degrees 45-50 minutes.** Serve with whipped cream.

BUTTERSCOTCH PIE

2 T. butter   1 cup fructose
2 eggs, separated   2 T. molasses
2 T. flour   1 baked pie shell
2 cups milk   meringue for topping

Beat egg yolks, stir in flour and all the milk but 4 T. Mix well and set aside. Put butter in saucepan and melt, stir in fructose, molasses and 4 T. milk. Cook 5 minutes, then add first mixture and stirring constantly, cook until thick. Pour into crust and cover with meringue made with 2 stiffly beaten egg whites. **Bake 10 minutes on 350 degrees.**
Note: If using sugar to replace fructose, use 2 cups brown and omit molasses.

The beauty of life is to be found in thoughts
that rise above the needs of self.

CHOCOLATE OATMEAL PIE

2 eggs
½ cup fructose
¼ tsp. salt
1 cup light corn syrup
2 T. butter, melted
1 unbaked pie shell

1 tsp. vanilla
½ c. unsweetened coconut
½ cup quick oats
½ cup unsweetened choc.
        chips.

Preheat oven to 350 degrees. Beat eggs about 5 minutes. Beat in fructose, salt, syrup, butter and vanilla. Stir in oatmeal, coconut and choc. chips. Pour into pie shell. **Bake 40-50 minutes.**
Note: If using sugar to replace fructose, use 1 cup.

COCONUT PIE

¼ cup fructose
3 T. cornstarch
¼ tsp. salt
2 cups milk
2 eggs, beaten

2 tsp. butter
1 tsp. vanilla
1 c. unsweetened coconut
1 baked 9" pie shell
whipped cream

Combine fructose, cornstarch and salt. Add milk and heat until thick. Stir in eggs and cook 1 more minute. Remove from heat and add vanilla, butter and coconut. Cool and pour into pie shell. Top with whipped cream.
Note: If using sugar to replace fructose, use ½ cup.

Christ can do wonders with a broken heart, if given all the pieces.

COCONUT CREAM PIE

Filling:
$1/3$ cup fructose	3 egg yolks, beaten
3 T. cornstarch	2 cups milk
dash of salt	1 tsp. vanilla
$3/4$ cup unsweetened coconut	1 9" baked pie shell

Combine fructose and cornstarch in saucepan. Slowly add milk and egg yolks. Cook over medium heat until thick. Remove from heat. Add vanilla. Sprinkle $1/2$ cup coconut in bottom of pie shell and add filling.

Meringue:
3 egg whites	$1/8$ cup fructose
$1/4$ tsp. cream of tartar	dash of salt
$1/4$ tsp. cornstarch	1 tsp. vanilla

Beat egg whites and cream of tartar until foamy. Add fructose, cornstarch, salt and vanilla; add to egg whites and beat until stiff peaks form. Spread over hot filling; sealing to edges. Sprinkle with remaining coconut. **Bake at 350 degrees 10 minutes.**
Note: If using sugar to replace fructose, use $2/3$ cup in filling and $1/4$ cup in meringue.

LEMON MERINGUE PIE

1 baked pie crust	$3/4$ cup realemon
3 eggs	2 T. cornstarch
4 egg yolks	$1/3$ cup butter
$1/2$ cup fructose	

Meringue:
4 egg whites	$1/2$ tsp. vanilla
$1/4$ tsp. cornstarch	$1/4$ tsp. cream of tartar
2 T. fructose	

For filling beat together eggs, egg yolks, fructose, realemon and cornstarch. Place in double boiler top and cook over simmering water. Do not boil. Cook until thickened, stirring constantly. Stir in butter and pour into baked pie crust.
For meringue, beat egg whites, cornstarch and cream of tartar. Add fructose and vanilla and beat until soft peaks. Put on filling sealing edges. **Bake at 350 degrees 10 minutes.**
Note: If using sugar to replace fructose, use 1 cup in filling and 3 T. in meringue.

OATMEAL BARS

¾ cup butter
¾ cup fructose
2 T. molasses
1 lg. or 2 sm. eggs
¼ cup water
1 cup unsweetened choc. or carob chips

¾ cup flour
1 tsp. salt
½ tsp. soda
3 cups quick oats
1 tsp. vanilla

Combine butter, fructose, molasses, egg, water and vanilla; mix well. Add rest of ingredients. **Bake at 350 degrees 20 minutes in greased pan.**
Note: If using sugar to replace fructose, use 1 cup firmly packed brown, ½ cup white and omit molasses.

GRANOLA BARS

½ cup fructose
½ cup honey
2 tsp. vanilla

⅔ cup peanut butter
½ cup butter or oleo

Mix all together until blended and stir in:
3 cups quick oatmeal
½ cup unsweetened coconut
1 cup unsweetened carob chips

½ cup raisins
⅓ cup wheat germ
½ cup sunflower seeds

Place mixture in greased 9"x13" pan. **Bake at 350 degrees 15-20 minutes.**
Note: If using sugar to replace fructose, use ¾ cup sugar and only ¼ cup honey.

Only one life, twill soon be past.
Only what's done for Christ will last.

SCOTCHEROOS

⅓ cup fructose
1 cup white corn syrup
1 cup peanut butter

6 cups rice crispies
1 cup unsweetened carob
    chips

Combine fructose and syrup in saucepan. Cook on medium until mixture boils. Remove from heat and add peanut butter. Mix well. Pour over rice crispies and stir in chips. Mix well. Spread in greased 9"x13" pan. Cool and cut into bars.
Note: If using sugar to replace fructose, use ⅔ cup.

UNBAKED PEANUT BUTTER BARS

¼ cup fructose
¾ cup peanut butter
1 cup unsweetened choc. chips

½ cup dark syrup
3 cups rice krispies

Heat fructose and syrup until melted. Add peanut butter and rice krispies. Press into 9" square pan. Melt chips over hot water and spread over bars and chill.
Note: If using sugar to replace fructose, use ½ cup.

CHOCOLATE BROWNIES

1 cup flour
½ tsp. soda
¾ cup fructose
1 stick butter
3 eggs

3 T. water
1½ cups unsweetened
    choc. or carob chips
1½ tsp. vanilla

In saucepan combine fructose, butter and water. Bring to boil over medium heat. Remove from heat. Stir in chips and vanilla until chips are melted and smooth. Cool completely. Stir in eggs and beat. Mix together flour and soda and add to batter. Pour into greased 9"x13" pan. **Bake at 350 degrees 30-35 minutes.**
Note: If using sugar to replace fructose, use 1 cup and add ¼ cup more flour.

CHOCOLATE OR CAROB BROWNIES

1 cup butter
1 tsp. vanilla
1 cup fructose
3 eggs
1 cup nuts, opt.

¾ cup cocoa or carob
    powder
¾ cup flour
½ tsp. salt

Mix all together. Pour into greased 8"x8" pan. **Bake at 350 degrees for 30 minutes.**
Note: If using sugar to replace fructose, use 2 cups and add ¼ cup more flour.

CAROB GRAHAM SQUARES

1 cup unsweetened carob or choc.
        chips
¼ cup butter

¼ cup light corn syrup
8 double graham cracker
    squares

Heat carob, syrup and butter until smooth. Crumble up crackers into mixture and mix well. Pour into foil-lined 8"x8" pan. Cool. Lift foil out of pan and cut into squares.

CHOCOLATE CHIP COOKIES I

1 cup honey
½ cup butter
½ cup shortening
2 eggs
1 tsp. vanilla
2 cups flour
1 cup quick oats

2 tsp. baking powder
½ tsp. soda
¼ tsp. salt
1 cup unsweetened choc.
    chips
½ cup nuts

Cream honey, shortening and butter until smooth. Beat in eggs, 1 at a time, and add vanilla. Combine flour, oats, baking powder, soda and salt. Mix well. Add both together and mix well. Stir in chips and nuts. Drop by heaping T. on greased sheet. **Bake at 350 degrees 12-15 minutes.**

56

CHOCOLATE CHIP COOKIES II

½ cup fructose 1 egg
1 T. molasses ¾ cup flour
½ cup butter ½ cup quick oats
½ cup peanut butter 1 tsp. soda
½ tsp. vanilla ¼ tsp. salt
1 cup unsweetened choc. or carob chips

Beat fructose, butter, molasses, peanut butter, vanilla and egg. Mix in flour, oats, soda and salt. Stir in chips. Drop by T. onto greased cookie sheets. **Bake at 350 degrees 10-12 minutes.** Note: If using sugar to replace fructose, use ½ cup white and ⅓ cup brown. Omit molasses and add ¼ cup more flour.

CHOCOLATE PEANUT BUTTER COOKIES

¾ cup flour 1 tsp. vanilla
½ tsp. soda ½ cup fructose
1 cup biscuit mix 1 T. molasses
5 T. butter ¾ cup peanut butter
6 T. unsweetened cocoa powder ½ cup milk
1 egg 1 cup quick oats

Preheat oven to 350 degrees. Mix flour, soda and biscuit mix; set aside. Melt butter and cocoa; stir until smooth. Cool. Add egg, vanilla, fructose, molasses and peanut butter. Alternately add milk and flour mixture. Add oats. Drop by T. on cookie sheets. **Bake 10-12 minutes.**
Note: If using sugar to replace fructose, use ½ cup white sugar, ¼ cup brown sugar and omit molasses.

Hate is sand in the machinery of life - love is oil

MOLASSES COOKIES

1 cup butter
2 cups flour
2 cups chopped walnuts

¼ cup molasses
½ tsp. salt

Cream butter, add molasses. Sift flour and salt. Add to creamed mixture. Shape into balls. **Bake at 350 degrees 20 minutes or until lightly browned.**

GINGER COOKIES I

1 cup molasses
1 cup sour milk
1 cup lard

1 tsp. soda
1 heaping T. ginger
flour to make soft dough

Mix together. Roll out and cut with cookie cutter. **Bake at 350 degrees 8-10 minutes.**

GINGER COOKIES II

2 cups hot water
2 cups molasses
6 cups flour
2 tsp. baking powder
3½ tsp. ginger

1 tsp. soda
1 tsp. salt
½ cup canola oil
1½ cups raisins

Combine hot water and molasses. Combine dry ingredients and add to molasses mixture. Add oil and raisins. Mix well. Drop by tsp. on greased cookie sheets. **Bake at 350 degrees 10-12 minutes.**

58

GINGER SNAPS

¾ cup fructose
¼ cup butter
¼ cup molasses
1 egg, beaten
1¾ cups flour

¼ tsp. salt
1 tsp. cinnamon
½ tsp. nutmeg
2 tsp. ginger
1½ tsp. soda

Cream fructose with butter; add molasses and egg. Combine dry ingredients and add to creamed mixture. Blend thoroughly. Drop by tsp. on ungreased cookie sheets. **Bake at 350 degrees 12-15 minutes.**
Note: If using sugar to replace fructose, use ½ cup brown sugar, 1 cup white sugar and add ¼ cup flour.

CARROT COOKIES

¼ tsp. soda
1 cup honey
1 cup grated carrots
2 slightly beaten eggs
2 cups flour
2 tsp. baking powder

¼ tsp. salt
1 tsp. cinnamon
2 cups quick oatmeal
1 cup chopped nuts
1 cup chopped raisins

Mix soda into honey. Add carrots and eggs. Mix and sift dry ingredients; add oatmeal, nuts and raisins. Combine with honey mixture. Drop onto greased cookie sheets. Flatten with a fork. **Bake at 350 degrees 8-10 minutes.**

ORANGE COOKIES

1¼ cups flour
1 tsp. baking powder
¼ tsp. soda
⅓ cup melted butter
½ cup unsweetened orange juice

2 tsp. orange peel
1 egg
1½ tsp. sweetener, opt.
⅓ c. unsweetened coconut
dash salt

Mix all together. **Bake at 400 degrees 10 minutes.**

NO-BAKE RICE KRISPIE COOKIES

½ cup melted butter
1½ cups chopped dates
½ cup fructose
1 egg

½ tsp. salt
½ tsp. vanilla
½ cup pecans
3 cups rice krispies

Add dates, fructose and egg to melted butter. Cook slowly. Stir until thick. Remove from heat and add remaining ingredients. Shape into small balls and roll in unsweetened coconut while still warm.
Note: If using sugar to replace fructose, use 1 cup.

PECAN DATE BITES

8 oz. pitted semisoft dates
¼ cup butter
2 T. honey
⅓ cup pecans

¾ c. unsweetened coconut
¼ cup water
1¼ cups rolled oats
½ tsp. vanilla

Combine dates, coconut, butter, water and honey. Cook over medium heat until mixture boils, stirring frequently. Reduce heat, cook 3-4 minutes mashing dates with a wooden spoon until thick and well-blended. Remove from heat. Stir in oats, pecans and vanilla. Spread ½" thick in waxed paper lined pan. Chill 1½-2 hours. Cut in squares. Freeze until firm.

PEANUT BUTTER HONEY BALLS

1 cup crunchy peanut butter
1 cup whole grain cereal flakes

½ cup honey
1½ cups dry milk powder

Crush cereal and mix all ingredients together thoroughly. Roll into 1" balls. Chill 30 minutes.

60

CAROB CAKE

1½ cups flour
¾ cup fructose
½ cup carob powder
½ tsp. salt
1 T. soda

1 egg
⅔ cup oil
1 cup buttermilk
1 cup boiling coffee
1 tsp. vanilla

Sift together flour, carob, fructose, salt and soda. Add egg, oil and buttermilk. Blend in coffee and vanilla. Pour into greased 9"x13" pan. **Bake at 350 degrees 30-35 minutes.**

Filling:
3 T. butter
½ cup fructose
1 cup nuts
1 cup milk

1 T. molasses
1 tsp. vanilla
5½ T. flour
2 beaten egg yolks

Combine all ingredients except vanilla and nuts in saucepan. Cook on medium until thick; stirring constantly. Remove from heat and add vanilla and nuts. Cool and spread on cooled cake. Chill.

Frosting:
3 T. butter
½ cup fructose

3 T. milk
¼ cup carob chips

Combine all but chips in pan and boil 2 minutes. Remove from heat. Add chips. Beat until thick and melted. Drizzle on cake. Note: For using sugar to replace fructose, use 1¾ cups in cake and add ½ cup more flour. Use 1 cup brown in filling and ¾ cup in frosting.

Let Christ's beauty shine through me,
for all the whole world to see.

TOLL HOUSE CREAM CHEESE CAKE

²/₃ cup fructose
2 eggs
²/₃ cup oil
2 tsp. vinegar
2 cups water
½ cup cocoa
2 T. vanilla

3 cups whole wheat flour
2 tsp. soda
8 oz. cream cheese
1 egg
2 T. fructose
choc. or carob chips

Blend together the first 9 ingredients. Pour into ungreased 9"x13" pan. Blend cream cheese, egg and 2 T. fructose together. Spoon onto cake. Then sprinkle choc. chips all over cake. **Bake at 350 degrees 45 minutes.**

DATE CAKE

1¼ cups boiling water
1 cup chopped dates
¾ cup butter
½ cup fructose
2 cups flour (can use whole wheat)

1 tsp. vanilla
½ tsp. salt
1 tsp. soda
1 T. cocoa
2 eggs

Pour water over dates. Cool to room temperature. Cream butter and fructose, add eggs and vanilla, beat well. Mix flour, soda, salt and cocoa together. Add alternately to creamed mixture with dates, beginning and ending with dry ingredients. Pour into greased 9"x13" pan.

Topping:
2 T. fructose   ½ cup chopped nuts
1 cup carob or choc chips
Mix and sprinkle over batter, press down lightly. **Bake at 350 degrees 25-30 minutes.**

62

CREAM PUFF CAKE

Crust:

1 cup boiling water	1 stick butter
4 eggs	1 cup flour

Bring water and butter to a boil; remove from heat and add flour and eggs. Mix well. Put into 9"x13" greased pan. **Bake at 400 degrees 25-30 minutes.** Middle will be puffed. Punch down all but edge around outside.

Filling:

1 8oz. pkg. softened cream cheese 2½ cups milk
2 boxes sugar-free instant vanilla pudding
Combine pudding mix, milk and cream cheese. Mix with mixer. Spread on crust. Top with whipped cream.

GINGERBREAD I

2 cups flour	1 egg
⅓ cup less 1 T. fructose	1 tsp. soda
1 cup molasses	1 tsp. ginger
¾ cup hot water	1 tsp. cinnamon
½ cup shortening	¾ tsp. salt

Mix dry ingredients. Add molasses, hot water, shortening and egg. Mix on low ½ minute. Scrape down bowl. Beat 3 minutes on medium. Pour into greased 9"x13" pan. **Bake at 325 degrees 35 minutes.** Do not overbake. Top with whipped cream if desired.
Note: If using sugar to replace fructose, use ⅓ cup sugar and increase flour by ¼ cup.

Let not your heart be troubled the Lord will see you through.

63

GINGERBREAD II

¼ cup fructose
¼ cup butter
¾ cup boiling water
1 cup molasses
1 egg

1¼ cups flour
½ tsp. cinnamon
½ tsp. ginger
½ tsp. salt
½ tsp. soda

Cream fructose and butter. Add water, molasses, egg and dry ingredients. Put into 7"x11" pan. **Bake at 350 degrees 45 minutes.**
Note: If using sugar to replace fructose, use ½ cup.

GINGERBREAD III

1 cup molasses
1 tsp. soda
2 cups flour
½ cup butter, softened

1 tsp. ginger
1 egg, beaten
¼ cup warm water

Stir together molasses and soda until it foams. Mix together egg, butter, ginger, warm water and molasses. Add flour and blend well. **Bake at 350 degrees 30 minutes.** Serve with whipped cream.

GINGERBREAD IV

1¾ cups flour
1 tsp. soda
¾ tsp. salt
1 tsp. ginger
1½ tsp. cinnamon
½ cup wheat germ

⅛ cup fructose
1 cup buttermilk
¾ cup molasses
⅓ cup oil
2 eggs, beaten

Combine dry ingredients. Add remaining ingredients and beat until smooth. Pour into greased 9"x9" pan. **Bake at 350 degrees 35-40 minutes or until done.** Serve with whipped cream.
Note: If using sugar to replace fructose, use ¼ cup and increase flour ¼ cup.

ICING

3 T. flour
½ cup milk
1 stick oleo

¼ cup fructose
1 tsp. vanilla

Combine flour and milk. Cook over low heat until thick, stirring constantly. Let cool. Can use double boiler. Beat oleo and fructose until creamy. Add cool flour mixture and beat at high speed 7 minutes. Add vanilla.
Note: If using sugar to replace fructose, use ½ cup.

NO-COOK ICING

1 egg white
½ cup fructose
¼ tsp. cream of tartar

¼ tsp. vanilla
½ cup boiling water

Combine all ingredients. Beat 5 minutes or until soft peaks form.
Note: If using sugar to replace fructose, use 1 cup.

CAKE ICING

2 egg whites, stiffly beaten   1 cup honey

Place honey in saucepan. Heat slowly to boiling. Cook to soft ball stage. Pour slowly into egg whites. Beat until holds its shape. Spread on cake.

CHOCOLATE ICING

1 7oz. pkg. choc. or carob chips   ½ cup dairy sour cream
pinch of salt

Melt chips; add sour cream and mix well.

CAROB FROSTING

3 T. butter, softened
2/3 cup dry milk
1/3 cup carob powder

1/4 cup honey
1/4 cup cream
1 tsp. vanilla

Cream together butter and dry milk. Stir in carob powder. Beat in remaining ingredients.

CREAM CHEESE ICING

8 oz. low calorie cream cheese, softened
1/2 cup plain lowfat yogurt

1 tsp. vanilla
1 tsp. realemon
2 tsp. honey

Blend cream cheese and yogurt. Stir in rest of ingredients and beat well.

PEANUT BUTTER ICING I

1 (8oz.) pkg. cream cheese,soft
1 cup chopped unsalted peanuts, opt.

1/2 c. creamy peanut butter
1/2 cup white syrup

Mix cream cheese and syrup until smooth. Add peanut butter and beat well. Spread on cooled cake. Garnish with chopped peanuts.

PEANUT BUTTER ICING II

2/3 cup water
2/3 cup fructose

3/4 c. chunky peanut butter

Mix water and fructose and boil 1 minute. Cool. Add peanut butter and whip until fluffy.
Note: If using sugar to replace fructose, use 1 1/3 cups.

FRUITCAKE

2 eggs	1/8 tsp. ginger
1/3 cup butter	1/8 tsp. nutmeg
1 T. molasses	2 T. cream
3 T. honey	1 cup raisins
1/2 cup flour	1 cup chopped dates
1/2 tsp. salt	6 oz. dried apricots,
1/2 tsp. baking powder	chopped
1 T. fructose	3 cups pecan halves

Cream butter, fructose, molasses, eggs and honey. Combine dry ingredients and add to creamed mixture alternately with cream. Beat in raisins, dates, apricots and pecans. Put into 2 greased and floured loaf pans. Place in middle of oven with pan of water on bottom. **Bake at 300 degrees 50-60 minutes or until done.** Cool. Store in refrigerator.
Note: If using sugar to replace fructose, use 3 T. brown and omit molasses.

CHEESECAKE

1 8" pie crust or graham cracker crust

2 eggs	8oz. cream cheese
1/4 cup fructose or 1/3 cup honey	1/4 cup dry milk
1 T. lemon juice	2 tsp. vanilla

Combine all ingredients and pour into pie shell. **Bake at 350 degrees 30 minutes.** Cool and top with favorite unsweetened thickened fruit.
Note: If using sugar to replace fructose, use 1/2 cup.

RHUBARB SHORTCAKE

Boil: 1 cup fructose   2½ cups water
Sift together:
2 cups flour   3 tsp. baking powder
1 tsp. salt   1 T. honey
Add: ½ cup shortening   ⅔ cup milk
Filling: 3 cups rhubarb   ¼ cup fructose

Boil water and fructose. Set aside. Mix together dough ingredients and roll out in rectangle. Spread filling ingredients on dough
and roll up as for jelly roll. Cut in slices and lay in greased 9"x13"
pan. Pour syrup over all. **Bake at 400 degrees 25 minutes.**
Note: If using sugar to replace fructose, use 2 cups in syrup and
½ cup in filling.

OATMEAL NUT CANDY

Mix together by hand:
1 cup oatmeal   ½ cup honey
½ cup sunflower seeds   1 cup chopped nuts

Roll into balls and place on buttered cookie sheet. Chill to set
and dip in ⅜ cup melted, unsweetened choc. or carob chips.

Main Dishes

Notes

_____

_____

_____

_____

_____

_____

_____

_____

_____

_____

_____

_____

BREAKFAST CASSEROLE

3 med. potatoes
6-8 slices bacon
¼ cup onion, chopped
1 cup grated cheese (your choice)

½ cup cottage
5 eggs, beaten
½ tsp. salt

Cook or steam potatoes until tender; peel and dice. Preheat oven to 350 degrees. Fry bacon, drain; reserve drippings. Lightly brown potatoes and onion in drippings. Remove from heat and add bacon, cheeses, eggs and salt. Turn into butter baking dish and **bake for 30-40 minutes or until set in center.**

AMISH CASSEROLE

2 lbs. hamburger
peas or corn
1 can cream of mushroom soup
1 can cream of chicken soup

½ lb. grated cheese
1 cup celery
1 8oz. bag noodles

Brown hamburger and precook noodles and celery. Add other ingredients. Spread bread crumbs on top. **Bake at 350 degrees 45 minutes.**

BROCCOLI CASSEROLE

2 pkg. frozen broccoli
1 can cream of chicken soup
1 can cream of mushroom soup

1 onion
1½ cups bread crumbs
4 oz. grated cheese

Layer in order given, all but cheese in casserole. **Bake at 350 degrees 30 minutes.** Cover with grated cheese. Return to oven and bake until browned.

BROCCOLI-CHEESE CASSEROLE

1½ cups quick-cooking rice
1 can cream of mushroom soup
1 cup cheddar cheese, grated

⅓ cup butter
1½ cups water
1 pkg. frozen broccoli

Combine water and butter; bring to a boil. Add broccoli and simmer 5 minutes. Add uncooked rice; cover and set aside 5 minutes. Stir in soup and cheese. **Bake at 325 degrees 40 minutes.**

BROCCOLI RICE CASSEROLE

1 pkg. frozen broccoli, cooked
2 T. butter
½ can mushroom soup

1 onion, chopped
2 cups cooked rice
4 oz. shredded cheese

Saute onion in butter. Add remaining ingredients and **bake at 350 degrees 20-30 minutes.**

CHEESEBURGER RICE CASSEROLE

1 lb. ground beef
1 sm. onion, chopped
1½ cups water
½ cup catsup
2 T. mustard

½ tsp. salt
⅛ tsp. pepper
1½ cups minute rice
1 cup shredded cheddar
cheese

Brown meat and onion; drain fat. Stir in water, catsup, mustard, salt and pepper. Bring to a boil. Stir in rice; cover. Remove from heat. Let stand 5 minutes. Fluff with fork. Sprinkle with cheese; cover. Let stand until cheese melts. Garnish with lettuce, pickle and tomato.

CHICKEN CASSEROLE I

1¼ cups broken spaghetti	1 cup cooked peas
2 cups cooked, diced chicken	½ tsp. salt
½ cup chopped onions	½ cup chicken broth
1 can cream of mushroom soup	1¾ cup grated cheese

Cook spaghetti; drain. Add remaining ingredients except 1 cup cheese; mix. Put in greased casserole dish and **bake at 325 degrees 1 hour.** Top with remaining cheese.

CHICKEN CASSEROLE II

4 cups chicken, cut up and cooked	1 cup bread crumbs
2 stalks celery	1 small onion
1 can cream of chicken soup	salt to taste

Place chicken, celery and onions in casserole dish. Put bread crumbs on top and chicken soup. **Bake at 350 degrees 30 minutes or until hot.**

CHICKEN CASSEROLE III

2 cups cooked chicken, cut up	½ cup milk
5 hard-boiled eggs	10-12 slices broken bread
1 can cream of mushroom soup	

Heat soup and milk. Combine with remaining ingredients. Pour into buttered casserole. **Bake at 350 degrees 30 minutes.**

CHICKEN CASSEROLE IV

2 cans cream of mushroom soup	2 cups uncooked macaroni
2 scant cups chicken broth	1 onion, chopped
2 cups cooked, diced chicken	1 c. cubed velveeta cheese

Mix all together and **bake at 350 degrees 1½ hours.**

CHICKEN RICE CASSEROLE

2 cups cooked rice
2 T. diced onion
2 cups cooked, diced chicken

¾ cup salad dressing
1 can cream of chicken
    soup

Cook rice and set aside. Mix all ingredients and place in 9"x13" baking dish. Top with:
2 T. melted butter   1 cup corn flakes, crushed
Bake at 350 degrees 1 hour.

CHILI MAC

1 lb. ground beef
1 sm. onion
1 pkg. taco seasoning
1 pkg. (7¼oz.) macaroni & cheese

1 can (8oz) tomato sauce
6 cups boiling water
2 tsp. salt
¼ cup water

Saute beef and onion until browned; drain. Stir in taco seasoning, ¼ cup water and tomato sauce. Simmer uncovered 15 minutes. Cook macaroni with water and salt and drain. Add macaroni and cheese mix to meat mixture. Mix well.

DRIED BEEF CASSEROLE

3 T. butter or oleo
3 T. flour
¾ cup light cream
1 cup liquid from peas
1½ cups dried beef, shred
2 cups canned peas

¼ tsp. pepper
3 cups cooked, sliced
    potatoes
1 tsp. salt
⅓ cup bread or cracker
    crumbs

Melt butter. Add flour, cream and liquid. Cook until thick, stirring constantly. Add dried beef, peas and pepper. Arrange potatoes in casserole, sprinkle with salt. Pour beef mixture over. Top with crumbs. **Bake at 375 degrees 20 minutes.**

74

GREEN BEAN CASSEROLE

¼ cup shredded cheddar cheese
1 can french fried onion rings

1 qt. green beans
1 can cream of mushroom
soup

Drain beans; save ¼ cup liquid and add to beans. Mix in undiluted soup and add cheese; stir. Put in baking dish. Just before baking add onion rings. **Bake at 350 degrees 30-35 minutes.**

HAM CASSEROLE I

1 cup chopped ham
3 lg. potatoes, sliced
2 carrots. sliced
1 sm. onion, sliced

salt and pepper to taste
1 can cream of celery soup
1 soup can milk

Arrange ham, potatoes, carrots and onions in 3 layers. Season with salt and pepper. Cover with combined soup and milk. **Bake at 400 degrees 1 hour.**

HAM CASSEROLE II

1 (10oz.) pkg. frozen broccoli
5 oz. spaghetti, cooked, drained
2 cups chopped, cooked ham

1lb velveeta cheese,cubed
1 cup milk
½ cup lite salad dressing

Cook and drain broccoli. Heat cheese, milk and salad dressing over low heat; stir until smooth. Add remaining ingredients; mix well. Pour into 2 qt. casserole. **Bake at 350 degrees 35-40 minutes.**

HAM, POTATO AND CHEESE CASSEROLE

3 cups hash brown potatoes   1 cup cottage cheese
1 3oz. pkg. cream cheese   2 cups chopped ham
1 cup shredded mozzarella cheese 1 T. chives
½ tsp. basil   ½ tsp. paprika

Combine cottage cheese, cream cheese, chives, basil and paprika. Mix well. In ungreased baking dish place ½ the hash browns. Spread cream cheese mixture on top; sprinkle ham evenly over top. Sprinkle half the mozzarella over. Top with remaining hash browns. **Bake uncovered at 375 degrees 35-40 minutes.** Top with remaining mozzarella. **Return to oven 2-3 minutes.**

HAMBURGER CASSEROLE I

1 lb. hamburger   ½ cup onion, chopped
½ cup celery,chopped   2 cups noodles
1 can tomato soup   ½ cup water
1 cup peas   ½ cup shredded cheese
salt and pepper to taste

Brown hamburger, onion and celery. Add remaining ingredients and spoon into 1½ qt. casserole. **Bake at 375 degrees 50 minutes or until noodles are tender.**

HAMBURGER CASSEROLE II

1 lb. hamburger   1 cup uncooked rice
1 onion   3 beef bouillon cubes
1 cup celery, uncooked   3 cups water
1 cup carrots   1 pkg. peas
1 can mushroom soup

Fry meat and onion. Dissolve bouillon cubes in water. Mix all together. **Bake at 300 degrees 1½-2 hours.**

HAMBURGER CASSEROLE III

1 lb. ground beef	1 can celery soup
1 onion	4 oz. grated cheese
16 oz. pkg. noodles	½ can chow mein noodles

Brown onions and beef together; drain. Cook noodles and drain. Mix together and spoon a layer into baking dish. Spread with layer of cheese. Continue to layer until all used. Cover with celery soup. **Bake at 350 degrees 30 minutes.** Remove and cover with chow mein noodles. **Bake 10 minutes more.**

HAMBURGER-GREEN BEAN CASSEROLE I

1 lb. hamburger	¾ cup milk
1 sm. onion, chopped	velveeta cheese to taste
3 potatoes, diced	salt and pepper to taste
1 can cream of mushroom soup	1 can green beans

Brown hamburger and onion together. Put on bottom of casserole dish. Season to taste. Add potatoes and beans and season to taste. Distribute cheese throughout layers. Mix soup and milk together and pour over all. **Bake at 350 degrees 1-1½ hours or until tender.**

Another person's secret is like another person's money;
you are not as careful with it as you are with your own.

HAMBURGER-GREEN BEAN CASSEROLE II

1 lb. ground beef
1 (9oz.) pkg. green beans, frozen
1 (10¾ oz.) can tomato soup
¼ cup water
½ cup shredded cheddar cheese

⅛ tsp. pepper
2 cups mashed potatoes
1 can Durkee french fried
          onions
½ tsp. salt

Cook and drain green beans. Fry beef and drain. Combine beef, beans, soup, water, salt and pepper. Pour into 1½ qt. casserole. Combine mashed potatoes and ½ can onions. Spoon mixture in a mounded ring around top outer edge of casserole. **Bake uncovered at 350 degrees 25 minutes.** Top with cheese and remaining onions and **bake 5 more minutes.**

HAMBURGER-NOODLE CASSEROLE

2 cans cream of mushroom soup
2 cans cream of chicken soup
1 soup can water

2 lbs. hamburger
1 lb. cheddar cheese
1 pkg. noodles

Fry hamburger; drain. Cook noodles; drain. Grate cheese and mix all together. **Bake at 350 degrees 1-1½ hours.** Serves 20.

PORK CASSEROLE

Brown 2½ lbs. cubed pork (rolled in 3T. flour) in 3 T. shortening. Add 1 cup water ¾ cup onion, 1½ cups celery, 1 tsp. thyme, ¾ tsp. salt, 2 tsp. kitchen bouquet and⅛ tsp. pepper. Cover and cook slowly 1 hour. Add 1lb.5oz. frozen mixed vegetables and 2 cans mushroom soup. Heat well. Top with biscuits.

Biscuits:
2½ cups flour
½ tsp. salt
½ cup shortening

½ tsp. margoram
1½ tsp. baking powder
1½ cups milk

Sift dry ingredients. Cut in shortening and add milk. **Bake at 350 degrees until biscuits are done.**

SAUSAGE CASSEROLE I

1 lb. sausage
2 cups cooked rice
¼ cup onion
½ cup celery
¼ cup green pepper
½ cup grated cheddar cheese

¾ cup milk
1 can mushrooms,
　　　　　　drained
1can cream of mushroom
　　　soup

Cook sausage until browned. Stir in remaining ingredients (except cheese). Pour into 2 qt. casserole dish and sprinkle with cheese. **Bake uncovered at 350 degrees 45 minutes.**

SAUSAGE CASSEROLE II

Brown: 1½ lbs. sausage and 1 sm. chopped onion
Cook: 8 oz. noodles and 1 tsp. salt in water
Heat together:　　　　1 can cream of chicken soup
　　　　　　　　　　　1 cup shredded cheese
　　　　　　　　　　　1 can milk
Combine all together. Top with buttered bread crumbs. Put in greased baking dish. **Bake at 350 degrees 40 minutes.**

ITALIAN SAUSAGE CASSEROLE

2 cups partially cooked
　　　　　macaroni
1 pkg. frozen peas
1 med. onion
2 cups cooked, sliced italian
　　　　　sausage

½ c. ripe olives, sliced
1½ cups milk
1 can cream of celery
　　　　soup
½ tsp. salt
½ cup cheddar cheese,
　　　　shredded

Combine all but cheese in 3 qt. casserole. **Bake at 350 degrees 50-60 minutes or until macaroni is tender.** Sprinkle on cheese and return to oven until cheese melts.

SAUSAGE RICE CASSEROLE

1 lb. sausage
¼ cup onion, chopped
1 cup cream of mushroom soup

1 cup instant rice
¾ cup water
½ cup celery, diced

Fry sausage and onion until browned; drain. Add celery and simmer 5 minutes. Add remaining ingredients and mix well. Place in greased 2 qt. baking dish. **Bake at 350 degrees 1 hour.**

SIX LAYER DINNER

3 med. potatoes
⅔ lb. carrots
2 onions
salt and pepper to taste

½ cup uncooked rice
1½ lbs. hamburger
1 qt. tomato juice

Dice potatoes, carrots and onions and layer in baking dish. Brown hamburger, drain and crumble on top. Sprinkle rice on and pour tomato juice over all. Season to taste. **Bake covered at 350 degrees 2 hours.**

TACO CASSEROLE I

3 cups macaroni, cooked
        and drained
1 cup shredded cheddar cheese
½ cup sour cream
¼ cup chopped green pepper

1 lb. hamburger
1 pkg. taco seasoning
1 (15oz.) can tomato
        sauce

Brown hamburger; drain. Stir in seasoning. Mix tomato sauce and pepper. Bring to a boil; remove from heat. Combine macaroni, ½ of cheese and sour cream. Place on botom of baking dish. Top with meat mixture and remaining cheese. **Bake at 350 degrees 30 minutes.**

TACO CASSEROLE II

1 lb. hamburger
1 pkg. taco seasoning
1 cup cooked rice
1½ - 2 cups chili beans
1 pkg. shredded mozzarella cheese

½ pkg. doritos
shredded lettuce
chopped tomatoes
taco sauce

Brown hamburger; add taco seasoning and mix as directed on pkg. Let simmer 10 minutes. Put in 9"x13" pan in layers in order given: rice, beans, cheese, hamburger and crushed chips. **Bake at 350 degrees 20 minutes.** Layer remaining ingredients to taste. Can serve with hot cheese sauce.

TATER TOT CASSEROLE

2 cans corn beef hash
2 cans mixed vegetables, drained

1 pkg. tater tots

Preheat oven to 350 degrees. Line sides and bottom of 10"x10" buttered casserole with hash. Put vegetables in center and top with tater tots. **Bake 30 minutes**

TUNA CASSEROLE

1 cup uncooked rice
1 can tuna, with juice
1 med. onion, chopped
½ cup oleo

½ cup grated cheese
½ tsp. salt or to taste
buttered bread crumbs

Cook rice. Add tuna, onion, oleo, cheese and salt. Mix well and turn into greased casserole. Top with buttered bread crumbs. **Bake at 350 degrees 20-30 minutes.**

TUNA - MAC

1 cup macaroni, uncooked
1 7oz. can tuna, drained
1 cup tomato sauce
½ tsp. salt

½ cup cottage cheese
¼ cup sour cream
1 sm. onion, minced

Cook macaroni and add remaining ingredients. Mix together 1 T. melted butter and ¼ cup bread crumbs. Sprinkle on top of casserole. **Bake at 350 degrees 30 minutes.**

TUNA NOODLE CASSEROLE I

3 cups cooked noodles
1 can cream of mushroom soup
½ cup grated cheddar cheese

4 hard-boiled eggs
7oz. can tuna
½ cup milk

Mix all ingredients; add more milk if desired. **Bake at 350 degrees 45 minutes.**

TUNA NOODLE CASSEROLE II

1 can cream of mushroom soup
½ cup buttered bread crumbs

⅓ lb. noodles
1 6oz. can tuna

Cook noodles in salted water. Add tuna and soup and pour into greased casserole. Top with buttered bread crumbs. **Bake at 350 degrees 40 minutes.**

The right temperature at home is maintained by
warm hearts, not hot heads.

TUNA NOODLE SUPREME

4½ cup noodles, uncooked
1 (12½ oz.) can tuna, drained
1 cup sour cream
1 cup lite mayonnaise
¼ cup onion, chopped

½ cup parmesan cheese
½ cup milk
1 tsp. Dijon mustard
2 cups chopped broccoli

Cook pasta; drain. Stir together sour cream, mayonnaise, parmesan cheese, milk and mustard. Salt and pepper to taste. Add hot pasta, tuna broccoli and mustard. Stir well. Place in 2 qt. baking dish. Cover and **bake at 350 degrees 40-45 minutes.**

VEGETABLE CASSEROLE

5 carrots, peeled, sliced
1 can cream of chicken soup
1 cup cracker crumbs

1 head cauliflower, broken
¾ cup milk
2 T. butter

Cook carrots and cauliflower in boiling water 10 minutes; drain. Place in greased 2 qt. baking dish. Combine soup and milk; stirring well. Pour over vegetables. Combine crumbs and butter. Sprinkle over all. **Bake at 350 degrees 30 minutes.**

ZUCCHINI CASSEROLE I

2 lbs. zucchini, peeled, cubed
¼ cup onion, chopped
½ cup cracker crumbs, fine
½ cup shredded cheese

½ lb. sausage or
     hamburger
2 eggs beaten
½ tsp. salt

Cook squash in boiling water for 10 minutes; drain and chop. Fry meat and onions until browned; drain. Combine squash, meat, cracker crumbs, eggs, salt and half of cheese. Place in shallow baking dish. Sprinkle with remaining cheese. **Bake at 350 degrees 30-40 minutes.**

ZUCCHINI CASSEROLE II

3 cups cubed zucchini
1½ tsp. salt
1 med. onion
½ green pepper
2 T. oil
1 lb. ground beef

2 cups toasted bread
crumbs
1 cup diced cheese
2 T. uncooked rice
1 can tomato soup
¾ cup water

Boil squash in 1½ cups water with 1 tsp. salt. Saute onion and pepper in oil; drain. Brown beef; drain. Mix all together and pour into baking dish. **Bake at 325 degrees 1 hour.**

STIR - FRY CASSEROLE

6 slices bacon
4 potatoes, sliced thin
1 bunch broccoli, sliced
3 carrots, sliced
½ cup celery, sliced
1 med. onion, chopped

1 lb. smoked or polish
sausage, cut
salt to taste
pepper to taste
1 sm. head cauliflower

In electric skillet fry bacon until crisp. Remove bacon and part of drippings. Add potatoes, carrots, celery, onions, broccoli and cauliflower to bacon drippings. Fry over medium heat. Salt and pepper to taste. When tender place pieces of sausage on top. Heat covered 12 minutes. Top with crumbled bacon.

The man who looks at life with the eyes of God
will be finding some worth in even the worst
people and some goodness everywhere.

CHICKEN STIR-FRY

$^1/_3$ cup orange juice
¾ cup chicken broth
2 T. oil
½ tsp. ginger (opt.)
1 gr. pepper, cut in strips
1 lb. skinless, boneless chicken
        breast

1½ T. cornstarch
2 T. soy sauce
1 garlic clove, minced
1 cup green beans
¾ cup onion, chopped
1 pkg. frozen california
        blend rice

Pound chicken and cut in strips. Combine orange juice and corn-starch and pour over chicken. Cover and chill 2-3 hours. Drain chicken and discard juice. In large skillet heat oil and add garlic and ginger. Add chicken and stir-fry 3-4 minutes. Add veg-etables and stir-fry until crisp tender 5-6 minutes. Stir in broth and soy sauce mixture. Serve over rice.

CHICKEN AND DRESSING

1 chicken, cut up
bread, broken in pieces
chicken broth to taste

1 sm. onion
1 egg, beaten

Cook chicken, cool and take off bone. Dry bread overnight. Add diced onion, egg and enough broth to moisten. Put meat in bot-tom of 9"x13" pan. Put dressing on top of chicken. **Bake at 350 degrees for 30 minutes.**

It is more difficult by far to mend a heart that
has been broken by angry words than it
would be to hold them back unspoken.

TURKEY A LA KING

1 med. onion
¾ cup celery, chopped
¼ cup gr. pepper, diced
¼ cup butter
¼ cup flour

1½ cups chicken broth
3 cups cubed turkey
¼ cup half and half
1 can sliced mushrooms

In skillet saute onion, celery and peppers in butter until tender. Stir in flour until paste forms. Gradually stir in broth. Bring to boil, boil 1 minute. Reduce heat; add cream, turkey and mushrooms. Heat through. May be eaten on biscuits or toast.

STROGANOFF

1½ lbs. ground chuck
1 can cream of mushroom soup
1 can cream of chicken soup
½ pint sour cream

1 lg. onion
1 tsp. garlic salt
4 oz. can mushrooms
noodles

Saute meat and onion. Add garlic salt. When meat is cooked, add soups and mix well. Add mushrooms. Remove from heat and stir in sour cream . Serve over noodles.

GROUND BEEF STROGANOFF

1 lb. ground beef
1 cup shredded carrots
½ cup onion, chopped
1 cup dairy sour cream

2 T. flour
1 tsp. salt
1 cup milk
6 T. chicken broth

Brown beef, carrots and onion together. Drain fat. Add flour and salt. Gradually add milk and broth. Stir and cook until thickened. Add sour cream and heat through. Serve over rice, baked or mashed potatoes.

PIZZA CASSEROLE

1 lg. pkg. mozzarella cheese
1 lg. can pizza sauce
1 can mushrooms
½ green pepper, chopped
1½ pkg. fancy macaroni

1½ lbs. sausage
1 med. onion, chopped
½ cup pepperoni, diced
¼ cup olives, diced
parmesan cheese

Brown and drain sausage. Boil macaroni and drain. Mix all together and pour into greased baking pan. **Bake uncovered at 350 degrees 20 minutes.** Top with parmesan cheese.

PIZZA MEATLOAF

1 lb. hamburger
1 egg
¼ cup pizza sauce
$1/3$ cup milk
1 tsp. salt

$1/8$ cup celery, chopped
$1/8$ cup onion, chopped
½ cup oatmeal
2 tsp. mustard
$1/8$ tsp. pepper

Mix all together and **bake at 350 degrees 1 hour.**

HAM LOAF I

¼ cup fructose
1 T. molasses
1 lb. ground pre-cooked ham
½ cup dry bread crumbs
½ cup milk

1 tsp. dry mustard
½ lb. ground lean pork
1 egg, slightly beaten
¼ tsp. pepper

Combine fructose, molasses and mustard in bowl and stir. Set aside. Combine remaining ingredients in large bowl. Mix and pat meat mixture into loaf pan. Spoon first mixture over meat and **bake until meat is done.**
Note: If using sugar to replace fructose, use ½ cup brown sugar and omit molasses.

HAM LOAF II

Grind together:
1½ lb. ham   1 lb. pork
Add:
1 cup cracker crumbs   ¹/₈ tsp. pepper
2 eggs   ½ tsp. mustard
1 cup milk   1 T. horseradish
¹/₃ tsp. salt
Mix all together and shape into loaf. Pour sauce over.

Sauce:
¹/₃ cup fructose   1 tsp. mustard
1 T. molasses   ½ cup water
½ tsp. paprika   2 T. vinegar

Bring to a boil. Simmer 5 minutes. **Bake at 350 degrees 75 minutes.** Baste.
Note: If using sugar to replace fructose, use ¾ cup brown sugar and omit molasses.

SALMON LOAF

2 cans pink salmon (pour off juice)   ¼ cup milk
2 cups crushed salted crackers   2 eggs

Mix salmon, eggs, crackers and milk. Make into a meatloaf. **Bake at 375 degrees for 45 minutes.**

JUICY CHICKEN BALLS

1 lb. hamburger   1 tsp. salt
1 cup water   1 cup oatmeal

Mix together and chill 30 minutes. Form into balls, roll in flour and brown on all sides. Cover with 1 can cream of chicken soup mixed with 1 can water. Simmer 20 minutes.

PORK CHOPS AND RICE

1 box Uncle Bens wild rice   1 can water
1 can mushroom soup   4-6 pork chops

Arrange pork chops in baking dish. Mix rice, soup and water. Pour over pork chops. **Bake at 350 degrees 1½ hours.**

CHICKEN PATTIES

¾ cup chopped onions   ⅓ cup bread crumbs
2 eggs, beaten   1 tsp. salt
2 T. milk   ⅛ tsp. pepper
4 boneless, skinless chicken breasts (grind in food processor)

Mix all ingredients and drop by T. in hot oiled skillet. Fry on both sides. Can put barbecue sauce on and eat in buns.

LIVER PATTIES

1 lb. liver   2 slices bacon
1 sm. onion   1 green pepper
1 tsp. salt   ⅛ tsp. pepper
2 T. flour   1 egg

Grind liver, onion and green pepper in meat grinder. Add beaten egg, salt, pepper and flour. Mix well. Drop with a spoon on a hot, greased griddle.

Seven days without prayer makes one weak.

SALISBURY STEAK

1½ lbs. ground beef
2 eggs
2 T. onion, chopped
6 T. crushed, cheese-flavored
            crackers
3¾ cups water
4 beef bouillon cubes

1 tsp. salt
½ tsp. pepper
8 oz. mushrooms
4 T. butter
6 T. flour
1 tsp. worcestershire
            sauce

Combine beef, eggs, crackers, onion, salt and pepper. Mix well. Shape into patties. Fry on each side and drain. Remove from pan. In same pan saute drained mushrooms in butter 2 minutes. Stir in flour and blend well. Add water and bouillon; cook until thckened. Add worcestershire sauce. Return patties to gravy and cook on low 10 minutes. Serve with mashed potatoes.

PEPPER STEAK

1 lb. round steak
1 cup red or gr. peppers, slice thin
1 clove garlic
½ tsp. ginger
¼ cup oil
1 T. cornstarch

1 cup onion, thin sliced
¼ cup soy sauce
2 stalks celery, slice thin
1 cup water
2 tomatoes, cut in wedges

Cut beef into thin strips. Combine soy sauce, garlic and ginger. Add beef. Toss and set aside. Heat oil in frying pan. Add beef mixture and heat over high until browned. Simmer until tender. Add vegetables and fry until tender-crisp, about 10 minutes. Mix cornstarch and water. Add to mixture and stir and cook until thickened. Add tomatoes and heat through.

BAR-B-Q STEAK

1½ T. worcestershire sauce
½ cup water
¼ cup vinegar
¼ cup green pepper
½ cup onion, chopped
¼ tsp. pepper

1 cup ketchup
1 T. mustard
1 T. fructose
½ T. molasses
½ tsp. salt
4 lbs. round steak

Combine all ingredients but steak in a saucepan. Bring to a boil and simmer 3 minutes on low heat. Pour hot sauce over steak. **Bake at 325 degrees 1½-2 hours.**
Note: If using sugar to replace fructose, use 2 T. brown sugar and omit molasses.

BARBECUED SPARERIBS

3-4 lbs. spareribs
2 onions
2 T. vinegar
2 T. worcestershire sauce
1 T. salt
¾ cup water

1 tsp. paprika
½ tsp. red pepper
½ tsp. black pepper
1 tsp. chili powder
¾ cup catsup

Cut ribs into servings. Sprinkle with salt and pepper. Place in roaster and cover with onion. Combine remaining ingredients and pour over ribs. Cover and **bake at 350 degrees 1½ hours.** Baste occasionally, turning once or twice. Remove cover last 15 minutes.

God is our refuge and strength. A very present help in trouble.

CHICKEN SUPREME

2 cups uncooked macaroni
2 cups chicken, cooked, diced
1 can cream of celery soup
4 hard boiled eggs
1 can cream of mushroom soup

½ lb. velveeta cheese,
cubed
2 cups milk
1 sm. onion, chopped

Mix all but eggs. Refrigerate overnight. Before baking mix in eggs. **Bake at 350 degrees 1 hour 15 minutes.** Let set 20 minutes before serving.

CHICKEN POT PIE

½ cup chicken broth
1 small onion
1 lg. garlic clove
¼ tsp. pepper
2 T. flour
½ tsp. salt

1 lb. skinless, boneless
chicken breast
3 sliced carrots
½ stick butter
1 cup frozen peas
1 cup milk

Topping:
½ cup cornmeal
½ cup flour
1 tsp. baking powder
¼ tsp. soda

1 egg
¾ cup buttermilk
1 T. oil

Pound chicken with tenderizer. Season to taste and broil a little on each side. Do not overcook or they will be tough. Set aside. Cook carrots and peas in a little water until tender, drain and set aside. In a skillet melt butter. Add onion, minced garlic, salt and pepper. Cook 5 minutes. Add flour and cook 1 minute. Stir in broth and milk and cook until thickened. Add carrots, peas and chicken (cut in pieces). Spoon into 1½ qt. casserole. Blend topping ingredients, stirring only until moistened. Spoon over chicken. **Bake at 400 degrees 30 minutes or until done.**

HOT SANDWICHES

½ lb. hot dogs   2 hard-cooked eggs
⅓ cup cheddar cheese
Grind all together and add:
3 T. chili sauce   1 tsp. mustard
2 T. relish   ½ tsp. garlic salt

Put in hot dog buns and wrap in foil. **Bake at 375 degrees for 20 minutes.** Serves 8.

BARBECUED WEINERS

½ cup onion   ½ cup catsup
1 tsp. worcestershire sauce   1 tsp. melted butter
1 tsp. pepper   2 T. vinegar
1 T. honey   2 tsp. mustard
any amount of weiners

Cook onion and butter until slightly brown. Add all but weiners. Mix well. Pour over weiners. **Bake at 350 degrees 25-30 minutes.**

VELVEETA SALSA MAC

½ lb. ground beef   1 8oz. jar salsa
1 7oz. pkg. macaroni, cooked,   1 lb. velveeta, cubed
                    drained

Brown meat; drain. Reduce heat to low. Add cheese, salsa and macaroni; stir until cheese is melted and macaroni is heated.

CHEDDAR BURGERS

1 lb. ground beef
1 cup grated cheddar cheese
½ cup bread crumbs
toasted sandwich buns

¼ cup minced onion
3 T. heinz 57 sauce
¼ tsp. salt

Mix all together and form into patties. Grill or broil until done.
Serve in buns.

CHICKEN BURGERS

2 cups cooked chicken, diced fine
1 cup dried bread crumbs
1 tsp. grated onion

½ tsp. salt
$\frac{1}{8}$ tsp. pepper
1 egg

Mix together well. Fry on medium heat in oil or butter. Turn
once. Serve in buns.

SLOPPY JOES I

1 lb. hamburger
2 chopped onions
2 T. flour
$\frac{1}{8}$ cup fructose
1 T. molasses

1 cup water
1 can corned beef
1 T. vinegar
1 cup ketchup

Fry hamburger and onion until browned. Add remaining ingredients and simmer 30 minutes.
Note: If using sugar to replace fructose, use ¼ cup brown sugar
and omit molasses.

SLOPPY JOES II

1½ lbs. hamburger ¾ cup chopped onions
Brown together in skillet and add:
1 cup celery 1½ T. fructose
¾ cup oatmeal 2 T. vinegar
1 cup milk 1 cup catsup
1 T. salt ¾ cup water
2 T. worcestershire sauce

Bake at 300 degrees for 1½ hours.
Note: If using sugar to replace fructose, use 3 T.

BARBECUE

1½ lbs. ground beef 1 onion, chopped
1 can corned beef 1 cup castsup
1 cup water 1 T. fructose
2 T. flour 1 T. molasses
1 T. chili powder

Fry beef and onion together. Drain fat. Add rest of ingredients
and simmer 15 minutes.
Note: If using sugar to replace fructose, use 2 T. brown and omit
molasses.

SPAM SALAD SANDWICHES

5 hard boiled eggs, shredded 1 can shredded spam
shredded cheese to taste 4 chopped dill pickles

Mix all together. Add lite salad dressing to taste. Spread on
bread.

POTATO CASSEROLE

6 lg potatoes
2 cups shredded cheese
¼ cup butter
4 tsp. chopped onion
paprika

1½ cups sour cream
1 tsp. salt
¼ tsp. pepper
2 tsp. butter

Cook potatoes with skins on. Cool, peel and shred. Over low heat, combine cheese and ¼ cup butter in saucepan, stirring until melted. Remove from heat. Blend in sour cream, onions, salt and pepper. Fold in potatoes and pour into 2 qt. greased casserole. Dot with 2 tsp. butter. Sprinkle with paprika. **Bake at 350 degrees 45 minutes.**

POTATO PUFF CASSEROLE

2 lbs. hamburger
1 pkg. peas

2 cans mushroom soup
1 pkg. tater tots

Fry hamburger and mix in mushroom soup. Put on bottom of roaster. Pour on 1 pkg. peas. Layer with slices of velveeta cheese, then tater tots on top. **Bake at 350 degrees 1-1½ hours.**

OVEN FRIED POTATOES

6 lg. potatoes
¼ cup oil
2 T. parmesan cheese
1 tsp. salt

½ tsp. pepper
½ tsp. garlic powder
1 tsp. paprika

Scrub potatoes well and cut in wedges lengthwise, leaving skins on. Combine rest of ingredients in a plastic bag. Add potatoes and shake to coat. Spread potatoes onto a cookie sheet in a single layer. **Bake uncovered in a 400 degree oven 25 minutes, stirring once.**

PAPRIKA POTATOES

½ cup butter
¼ cup parmesan cheese
6 potatoes, peeled, quartered
pinch of garlic or onion salt

¼ cup flour
1 T. paprika
⅛ tsp. pepper
¾ tsp. salt

Melt butter in 13"x9" pan. Combine next 6 ingredients in a large plastic bag; set aside. Rinse potatoes under cold water; drain well. Place half the potatoes in the bag; shake well to coat. Place in single layer in pan. Repeat with remaining potatoes. **Bake uncovered at 350 degrees 50-60 minutes.**

CREAM CHEESE POTATOES

4 med. potatoes
6 T. cream or milk
2 T. butter

1 6oz. pkg. cream cheese
1 tsp. salt

Cook potatoes in water until tender; drain. Beat cream cheese until fluffy. Gradually add potatoes mashing and beating until light. Add remaining ingredients and heat through. Serve hot.

MASHED POTATO HOT DISH

2 lbs. hamburger
4 T. shortening
4 cups tomato juice (2 cans)
3 cups green beans
½ tsp. pepper

1½ cups mild cheese,
                grated
4 cups mashed potatoes
1 cup finely chopped
                onion

Brown hamburger and onion in shortening. Add tomato soup, green beans and seasonings. Pour into greased casserole. Fold cheese into potatoes. Arrange on top of casserole. **Bake at 350 degrees 30-40 minutes.** 14-16 servings.

BAKED MASHED POTATOES

4 lg. potatoes   1 cup sour cream
¼ cup milk   1 pkg. cream cheese
½ tsp. salt   onion to taste
1 T. butter, melted

Cook potatoes until tender. Drain. Place in a large bowl and add milk, salt and butter. Beat until light and fluffy. Fold in sour cream, cream cheese and onion. Place in greased 1½ qt. casserole dish. **Bake at 350 degrees 20-30 minutes.** Can be made ahead and refrigerated.

CRUNCHY CHEESE POTATOES

Combine:
1 cup sour cream   ½ tsp. salt
1½ cups milk   ¼ tsp. pepper
Add: 6 med. potatoes, peeled and sliced thin.
Spread in baking dish.
Combine:
1 cup shredded cheddar cheese
½ cup finely crushed cornflakes
Sprinkle on top. **Bake at 350 degrees 50-60 minutes.**

POTATO WEDGES

4 med. potatoes, unpeeled   ½ tsp. salt
1 T. oil   2 garlic cloves, minced
¼ tsp. pepper

Cut potatoes in large wedges. Cover with cold water and let set 15 minutes. Drain potatoes and dry well. Sprinkle with oil, salt and pepper. Spread on greased cookie sheet. **Bake at 400 degrees for 20 minutes.** Turn potatoes and sprinkle with garlic. **Bake 20 minutes more.**

CANDIED SWEET POTATOES

2 or 3 sweet potatoes
pinch of salt
1 cup orange juice
3 T. butter

$^1/_8$ - ¼ cup fructose
1 T. molasses
1 T. cornstarch

Mix all but potatoes. Cook until thick. Pour over cooked, peeled sweet potatoes. **Bake at 350 degrees 15-20 minutes.**
Note: If using sugar to replace fructose, use $^1/_3$ cup white, $^1/_3$ cup brown and omit molasses.

BAKED BEANS I

2 (16oz.) cans pork and beans
3 T. flour
2 T. fructose
1 T. molasses
3 T. vinegar
1 onion, browned in bacon fat

1 cup tomato juice
¼ tsp. salt
1 can tomato sauce
1 lb. bacon, fried
2 T. barbecue sauce

Mix all together and **bake at 350 degrees 1 hour.**
Note: If using sugar to replace fructose, use 4 T. brown sugar and omit molasses.

BAKED BEANS II

2 (1lb.13oz.) cans pork and beans
2 med. onions, chopped
2 tsp. worcestershire sauce
½ cup fructose

1 lb. lean bacon, cut up
2 gr. peppers, chopped
1 cup catsup
1 T. molasses

Combine all together and **bake at 325 degrees 3 hours.** Uncover last 30 minutes.
Note: If using sugar to replace fructose, use 1 cup brown and omit molasses.

BARBECUED BEANS

1 (1lb.12oz.) can pork and beans
½ cup onion
1 T. worcestershire sauce
¼ tsp. pepper

1 lb. ground beef
½ cup catsup
½ tsp. salt
2 T. vinegar

Brown beef and onion; drain. Add remaining ingredients and mix well. Pour into baking dish. **Bake at 350 degrees 30 minutes.**

ESCALLOPED CORN

1 pint corn
1 tsp. salt
3 T. butter, melted
dash of pepper

¾ cup crushed cracker
          crumbs
2 eggs, beaten
1¼ cups milk

Preheat oven to 350 degrees. Mix all together and put in 1½ qt. buttered casserole. **Bake 1 hour.**

CRUSTY CORN

Melt 1 stick butter. Stir in:
1 can whole kernel corn
1 (8½oz.) pkg. jiffy corn muffin mix

1 can cream style corn
1 (8oz.) tub sour cream

Bake in 9"x13" pan at 350 degrees 40-45 minutes.

Prayers should be the key of the day and the lock of the night

---

STUFFED GREEN PEPPERS

4 green peppers
½ lb. hamburger
1 cup cooked rice
¼ cup onion

1 tsp. salt
⅛ tsp. pepper
1 8oz. can tomato sauce

Cut peppers in half lengthwise; remove seeds and wash. Combine all but ½ can tomato sauce. Place peppers in baking dish and fill each with meat mixture. Pour remaining sauce over peppers. Cover tightly and **bake at 350 degrees 1 hour and 15 minutes basting occasionally.**

SPANISH RICE

1 lb. ground beef
1 med. onion, chopped
1 gr. pepper, chopped
1 can (14½oz.) stewed tomatoes
1½ cups water
1 cup uncooked long grain rice

1 tsp. salt
1 tsp. chili powder
½ tsp. basil
¼ tsp. pepper
½ tsp. thyme
2 T. tomato paste

Cook ground beef, onion and green pepper until browned; drain. Stri in all but tomato paste; bring to a boil. Reduce heat, cover and simmer 20 mintues or until rice is tender. Stir in tomato paste and heat through. Serve with french bread.

The golden rule of friendship is to listen
to others as you would have them listen to you.

CHILI ENCHILADAS

1 lb. hamburger
chopped onion
2 cups pinto beans, with juice
½ tsp. salt
dash of pepper

2-3 tsp. chili powder
1 cup grated cheese
tomato juice
tortillas

Saute ¼ cup onion and hamburger. Add beans and seasonings. If mixture is dry, add tomato juice to make it sloppy. Simmer. Fill tortillas with about ¾ cup hamburger mixture. Sprinkle with 1 tsp. onion and 1 tsp. grated cheese. Roll up. Place in flat baking dish. Spoon remaining chili mixture over top. Sprinkle with chopped onion and cheese. **Bake at 350 degrees, uncovered for 20 minutes or until cheese melts.**
Variations: Make pizza enchiladas by adding pizza sauce to hamburger mixture and omitting chili powder. Pepperoni may be place inside each tortilla. Sprinkle with olives and mushrooms. Taco enchiladas can be made by adding taco seasoning to beef. Sprinkle with olives. Serve with lettuce, tomato and sour cream.

PIZZA ROLLS

2 tubes refrigerator biscuits   2 c. shredded mozzarella
Combine or use prepared pizza sauce:
1 8oz. can tomato sauce   1½ tsp. dried oregano
1 tsp. dried basil   ⅛ tsp. garlic powder

Roll or pat biscuits flat (2½") circles. Place on greased cookie sheets. Put small amount of sauce and cheese on half of biscuit. Fold over and seal edges with fork. **Bake at 400 degrees 8-10 minutes.** Makes 20 rolls.

Soups and Salads

Notes

_____

_____

_____

_____

_____

_____

_____

_____

_____

_____

_____

POTATO SOUP

Saute ½ cup finely chopped onion in 2 T. oil. Add 2 T. flour, 2 tsp. salt and pepper to taste. Add 2 cups water and blend well. Bring to boil and cook 1-2 minutes stirring constantly. Add 2 cups mashed potatoes and 4 cups milk. May add 1 cup grated cheddar cheese. Heat slowly.

GOLDEN POTATO SOUP

6 cups potatoes
2 cups water
1 cup diced carrots
1 cup diced celery

½ cup diced onion
2 tsp. chicken bouillon
1 tsp. salt
¼ tsp. pepper.

Bring to boil. Reduce heat and simmer until tender. Mix together ¼ cup flour and ¼ cup milk. Stir into soup. Add 2¾ cups milk and 1 cup shredded cheese. Heat through.

TUNA-POTATO SOUP

1 (6½oz.) can chunk light tuna
1 can cheddar cheese soup/sauce
seasoning to taste

2⅓ - 3 cups milk
3 med. potatoes
3 med. carrots

Dice the potatoes and carrots and boil 10 minutes or until soft. Melt the cheese in the milk at a low temperature. Add tuna to the milk, and add potatoes and carrots. Add seasoning to taste. Simmer 5-10 minutes.

Peace rules the day when Christ rules the world.

POTATO CHOWDER

4 cups diced potatoes
½ cup chopped onions
1 cup grated carrots
1 tsp. salt
¼ tsp. pepper

1 T. parsley flakes
4 chicken bouillon cubes
6 cup scalded milk
4 T. butter
½ cup flour

Combine potatoes, onion, carrots, salt, pepper, parsley and bouillon. Add enough water to cover. Cook until tender. Do not drain. Scald milk. Remove 1½ cups milk and combine with butter and flour. Return to milk. Cook until thickened and add to potatoes.

TOMATO SOUP

2 T. butter
Saute and blend in:
3 T. flour
1 tsp. salt
dash of garlic salt, basil, oregano

2 T. onion

2 tsp. honey
¼ tsp. pepper

Remove from heat and stir in 2 cups tomato juice. Boil 1 minute. Stir in 2 cups milk. Heat and serve.

CANNED TOMATO SOUP

6 onions
1 bunch celery, chopped
8 qts. tomatoes, quartered
⅓ cup honey

¼ cup salt
1 cup flour
1 cup butter

Blend onions and celery in blender. Add to tomatoes. Cook until tender. Put through sieve. Return juice to kettle and add butter and salt. Make paste of honey, flour and a little water. Add to juice. Simmer until slightly thickened. Put in jars and process 15-20 minutes.

CHICKEN SOUP

4 cubes chicken bouillon   1 cup diced celery
1 med. onion
Cook together 20 minutes and cover.
Add:
2½ cups diced raw potato   1-20oz. pkg. california blend
Cook 30 minutes.
Add:
2 cans cream of chicken soup   1 lb. velveeta cheese, cubed
Stir until blended.

CHICKEN RICE SOUP

1½ cup chicken broth   ½ cup carrots
3 cups cold water   ¾ lb. velveeta cheese
½ cup uncooked rice   1½ cups cooked, diced
½ cup celery   chicken

Combine first 5 ingredients. Cover and simmer 25 minutes. Add remaining ingredients. Stir until cheese melts.

CHICKEN NOODLE SOUP

2 cups chicken   2 T. minced onion
2 cups chicken broth   ½ cup grated carrots
1 qt. water   2 tsp. salt
2 chicken bouillon cubes   1 T. parsley
2 cups uncooked noodles

Simmer all together until noodles are soft.

GOLDEN SOUP

½ cup onion, chopped
½ cup celery, chopped
2 T. butter
2 cup chicken broth
2 cups sliced mushrooms

1 tsp. salt
2 cups blended pumpkin
                    or squash
2 cups milk
½ cup uncooked rice

Saute onion and celery in butter. Add broth, mushrooms, rice and salt. Bring to boil. Cover and simmer until rice is tender about 20 minutes. Stir in pumpkin and cook 5 minutes. Stir in milk and heat through.

CREAM OF PEA SOUP

2 cups frozen peas, thawed
1 small onion
3½ cups milk

2 chicken bouillon cubes
3 T. flour
salt and pepper to taste

Blend all together until smooth. Heat slowly stirring constantly. More milk may be added if desired.

CAULIFLOWER SOUP I

Cook until soft: 1 head cauliflower
Saute:
4 T. butter   ¼ cup chopped onion
Add: ¼ cup flour
Add:
3 cups chicken broth   cauliflower (with cooking
2 cups milk   water)

Cook until mixture thickens slightly. Add 1 cup shredded cheddar cheese. Heat and serve.

CAULIFLOWER SOUP II

1 head cauliflower
4 T. butter
1 med. onion
1 tsp. worcestershire sauce

¼ cup flour
3 cups chicken broth
1 cup shredded cheese
1 cup milk

Chop cauliflower and cook in salted water. Saute onion and butter in saucepan. Blend in flour. Gradually add broth and milk. Add cauliflower and worcestershire sauce. Cook until thickened. Stir in cheese.

CAULIFLOWER-BROCCOLI SOUP

1 (1lb.) pkg. frozen cauliflower-broccoli
2 chicken bouillon cubes
1 small onion
1 cup milk
½ cup grated cheddar cheese

1 tsp. salt
water to cover
3 T. cornstarch

Combine vegetables, bouillon, salt, onion and enough water to cover. Cook over low heat until vegetables are tender. Dissolve cornstarch in milk and add to soup. Stir and heat until thickened. Add cheese.

BEAN SOUP

2 cups navy beans
1 hambone
2 stalks celery
1 qt. tomato juice

2 qts. water
2 sm. onions, chopped
2 carrots, grated
salt and pepper to taste

Soak beans and water overnight. Add remaining ingredients and simmer 2-3 hours or until beans are tender.

FAVORITE BEAN SOUP

1 lb. navy beans
1 lg. carrot, diced
1 lg. onion, diced

1 cup celery, sliced thin
12 cups water
1 med. size potato, diced

Soak beans overnight in the water. Add all ingredients as listed and bring to boiling. Reduce heat and simmer 2½ hours or until beans are tender. Serve with biscuits.

SPLIT PEA SOUP

1 lb. dried split peas
1 ham bone or chopped ham
1 grated carrot
1 med. onion, chopped

4 cups chicken broth
4 cups water
salt and pepper to taste
1 cup diced, raw potatoes

Soak peas overnight. Drain water. Add all ingredients. Cook 4-5 hours over low heat, stirring occasionally. Can use slow cooker 8-10 hours on low. Serves 8-10.

BEEF BARLEY SOUP

2 lbs. boneless, cubed beef
2 T. oil
1½ cups med. barley
1 cup onions, chopped
3 carrots, diced

16 oz. tomatoes, cut
3 stalks celery, chopped
2 tsp. pepper
¼ cup parsley

In dutch oven, bring beef and 10 cups water to a boil. Skim off foam, cover and let simmer 1 hour. Add remaining ingredients stirring occasionally. Simmer uncovered 1 hour or until meat and barley are tender. Serve immediately. Serves 12.

CANNED VEGETABLE SOUP

1 pk. tomatoes, peeled
1 qt. lima beans
6 ears sweet corn, cut off cob
1 lg. cabbage head
½ cup salt, scant

1 bunch celery
2-3 peppers
4 lg. onions
6 lg. carrots

Cut tomatoes and cabbage coarse. Dice carrots and celery. Add beans whole which have been cooked until almost tender. Mix all together and cook 20 minutes. Cold pack 90 minutes. When opened to use, add 1 qt. water, fresh cooked potatoes, fried hamburger and butter.

STEW

1½ lbs. cubed beef
¾ cup chopped onion
seasonings to taste

diced potatoes to taste
diced carrots to taste

Brown beef and onion until soft. Cook potatoes and carrots in anoth pan; drain. Take juice from beef and make gravy. Mix all together and heat through.

BEEF STEW I

1 lb. stew meat
4 med. potatoes, cut up
1 can tomato sauce
½ tsp. pepper

4 med. carrots, sliced
1 cup beef broth
½ tsp. salt
¼ cup onion

Combine all ingredients and cook until tender.

BEEF STEW II

1 lb. cubed beef
2 T. flour
3 tsp. oil
2 lg. onions, chopped
2 cups mushrooms, opt.
2 garlic cloves, minced

2 tsp. tomato paste
2 cups beef broth
4 cups sliced carrots
2 med. potatoes, cubed
1 cup green bean pieces
1 T. cornstarch

Coat beef with flour and brown in oil over medium heat. Remove beef from pan and add onions, mushrooms and garlic. Saute; stirring 1 minute. Pour off oil. Add beef, tomato paste and broth. Add enough water to cover. Bring to boil; simmer 1¼ hours. Add carrots, potatoes and green beans. Simmer until tender. Mix cornstarch with 1 T. water and stir into stew. Boil 1 minute.

CHEESE SOUP

½ cup celery, diced
1 cup onion, diced

1 cup carrots, diced
1 cup potatoes, diced

Boil together in 1 qt. water 20 minutes.

Add:
1 pkg. california blend
4 chicken bouillon cubes
2 cans cream of chicken soup

1 cup water
2 cups cubed velveeta

Heat until cheese melts.

POTATO CHEESE SOUP

5 potatoes, peeled, diced
½ cup celery, chopped
½ cup onion, chopped
1 qt. water
¼ tsp. pepper

2 T. butter
½ cup grated cheddar
                    cheese
1 T. parmesan cheese
1 T. salt

Cook potatoes, celery and onion with water until tender. Add seasonings, butter and cheese. Cook on low 15 minutes. Add parmesan.

BROCCOLI CHEESE SOUP

2 cans cream of chicken soup
2 cups grated cheddar cheese
1 sm. onion

2½ cups water
20 oz. frozen broccoli

Simmer water, broccoli and onions 20 minutes. Add soup and cheese; heat through.

CAULIFLOWER CHEESE SOUP

1 sm. head cauliflower
3 med. potatoes
2 carrots
1 onion
1 cup frozen peas

1 can cheddar cheese soup
1 can cream of mushroom
                        soup
1 soup can milk
1 tsp. salt

Cut up cauliflower. Dice potatoes, carrots and onion. Add peas and salt and cook in enough water to cover, until tender. Do not drain. Add soups and milk. Heat through.

CHILI I

1 lb. hamburger
1 med. onion
1 can tomato soup
1 pint tomato juice
salt and pepper to taste

1 can chili beans
1 T. honey
1 T. molasses
1 tsp. chili powder

Brown hamburger and onion. Add rest of ingredients. Add water if too thick.

CHILI II

1 lb. ground beef	1 qt. tomato juice
1 med. onion	1 tsp. salt
1 can chili beans	1-2 tsp. chili powder

Brown beef and onions; drain. Add rest of ingredients and simmer 1 hour.

JELLO SALAD

1 sm. pkg. unsweetened orange jello
1 lg. small curd cottage cheese
1 lg. can unsweetened crushed pineapple, drained
2 cups whipped cream

Combine dry jello and cottage cheese. Add pineapple and whipped cream. Mix well and refrigerate.

ORANGE JELLO

1 pkg. sugar-free orange jello	¼ cup fructose
1 can unsweetened crushed pineapple	2 cups whipped cream
	5 T. milk
1 8oz. pkg. cream cheese, soft	

Bring pineapple and fructose to a boil. Add jello and let cool until almost set. Mix cream cheese with milk, then add whipped cream. Stir into pineapple mixture. Chill.
Note: If using sugar to replace fructose, use ½ cup.

CRANBERRY RELISH

4 cups raw cranberries   1 orange, unpeeled
4 lg. apples, unpeeled   1 cup fructose

Grind fruit. Add fructose and mix well. Keeps well in refrigerator.
Note: If using sugar to replace fructose, use 2 cups.

CRANBERRY SALAD

2 cups cranberries, cooked and put through sieve
1 cup fructose   2 cups water
Add:
¼ cup fructose   2 pkgs. knox gelatin
When starts to gel add:
1 cup unsweetened crushed pineapple
1 cup white seeded grapes
nuts if desired
Top with whipped cream.
Note: If using sugar to replace fructose, use 2 cups and ½ cup.

COTTAGE CHEESE SALAD

unsweetened pineapple to taste   16 oz. cottage cheese
lg. box sugar-free jello, dry   grapes to taste
2 cups whipped cream   oranges to taste

Mix well and refrigerate.

CHERRY SALAD

2 (3oz.) pkg. sugar-free cherry jello
3 cups boiling water
1 can lite cherry pie filling
1 (8oz) pkg. cream cheese
1 (12oz) can unsweetened crushed pineapple, drained

Dissolve jello in water. Chill until partly set. Fold in pie filling and chill until firm. Mix cream cheese and pineapple and spread over top.

LEMON SALAD

2 cups hot water
2 pkgs. sugar-free lemon jello
4 oz. cream cheese
1 cup evaporated milk
1 can pineapple (unsweetened, 1 c. juice and 1½ cups crushed)

Mix hot water and jello; let set in refrigerator until almost firm. In another bowl, beat cream cheese and milk until whipped. Mix with jello mixture. Add pineapple and juice. Chill until firm.

LEMON-PINEAPPLE SALAD

1 sm. box lemon sugar-free jello
½ cup cold water
1 cup hot water
1 sm. can unsweetened crushed pineapple

Mix all together and let thicken. Add 1 cup whipped cream and ½ cup grated cheese.

ORANGE-PINEAPPLE SALAD

1 T. unflavored gelatin	1 cup cold water
2 T. honey	2 T. frozen orange juice
2 oranges, peeled and diced	1 sliced banana

1 cup unsweetened pineapple chunks and juice and water to make 1¼ cups

Combine gelatin and cold water in saucepan. Add honey and warm until gelatin is dissolved. Add orange juice and pineapple juice and water. Chill until syrupy and fold in oranges, banana and pineapple. Chill until set.

PINE-APPLESAUCE SALAD

1 sm. pkg. sugar-free lemon jello	2½ cup unsweetened crushed pineapple
1 sm. pkg. sugar-free strawberry jello	
2 cups hot water	2 cups unsweetened applesauce
1 T. lemon juice	

Dissolve each pkg. of jello separately in 1 cup hot water. Cool. Stir pineapple and lemon juice into lemon jello. Pour into 8"x8" pan and set aside to chill. Mix applesauce into strawberry jello. Cool, but do not chill. When lemon layer is firm, spoon strawberry jello on top. Chill until firm. Top with whipped cream.

PINEAPPLE SALAD

1 can unsweetened chunk pineapple
Cook until thick:

pineapple juice	2 eggs, well beaten
1 T. cornstarch	¼ cup fructose

Cool and add pineapple, grapes and 1 cup whipped cream.
Note: If using sugar to replace fructose, use ½ cup.

RASPBERRY SALAD I

1 cup hot water
1 pkg. sugar-free raspberry jello
1 pkg. frozen raspberries
1 cup unsweetened applesauce

1 small can unsweetened crushed pineapple, drained

Combine ingredients in order given and let thicken.

RASPBERRY SALAD II

1 lg. box sugar-free raspberry jello
2 cups unsweetened applesauce

1½ cups fresh or frozen raspberries
2 cups hot water

Mix hot water and jello. Let dissolve and add remaining ingredients and chill to thicken.

STRAWBERRY SALAD

1 (6oz.) box sugar-free strawberry jello
1 qt. frozen strawberries

1 can unsweetened crushed pineapple
2 cups boiling water

Mix water and jello until dissolved. Add strawberries; stir until berries are thawed. Add pineapple, including juice. Chill until set.

FRUIT COMPOTE

1 cup fresh strawberries, sliced
½ cup fresh or frozen blueberries
1 c. unsweetened pineapple chunks

½ cup fresh peaches, sliced
1 cup orange juice

Mix all together and chill.

118

SOUR BEAN SALAD

1 can green beans
1 can kidney beans
1 cup celery, sliced thin
½ cup fructose
½ cup oil

1 can yellow beans
1 green pepper
1 med. onion, sliced thin
1 cup vinegar
½ tsp. salt

Dissolve fructose in vinegar and oil, heat. Add salt and pour over rest of ingredients. Leave in refrigerator overnight.
Note: If using sugar to replace fructose, use 1 cup.

SUMMER BEAN SALAD

1 (15-16oz.) can pork and beans
1 cup cubed cheese
4 hard boiled eggs, chopped
½ cup chopped onions
½ cup chopped celery

½ cup chopped carrots
2 tsp. lite mayonnaise
1 tsp. mustard
1 tsp. salt
½ tsp. pepper

Mix all together and chill.

BROCCOLI SALAD

1 head broccoli, cut fine
6 hard cooked eggs, diced
ham or bacon to taste, cut
Dressing:
¾ cup lite salad dressing
½ T. fructose or honey

cauliflower to taste, cut fine
cheese to taste, diced

2 T. vinegar
½ cup milk

Add all ingredients. Mix dressing and pour over salad and mix well.
Note: If using sugar to replace fructose, use 1 T.

LAYERED LETTUCE SALAD

1 head lettuce
4 hard cooked eggs
8 slices bacon, fried and diced

1 cup celery, diced
1 pkg. frozen peas
1 onion, diced

Tear lettuce in pieces and place in 9"x13" glass pan. Arrange in order on top of lettuce. Mix together 1 T. fructose and 2 cups light salad dressing. Spread over top. Top with grated cheese. Refrigerate 8-12 hours.
Note: If using sugar to replace fructose, use 2 T.

MACARONI SALAD

3 cups cooked macaroni
        (1½ cups dry)
4 hard cooked eggs, grated
1 (6½ oz.) can tuna, drained

¼ cup diced celery
1 cup grated cheese
1 pt. canned peas,
        drained

Mix all together. Mix dressing ingredients and mix all together. Chill.
Dressing:
1 cup lite salad dressing
½ tsp. salt

2 T. mustard

PASTA SALAD

½ cup lite salad dressing
¼ cup parmesan cheese
2 T. milk
1½ cups cubed ham
½ tsp. salt

1 cup shell macaroni,
        cooked, drained
1 cup chopped tomato
1 c. green pepper chunks
¼ cup chopped onion

Combine salad dressing and cheese. Add milk and mix well. Add remaining ingredients and mix lightly. Chill several hours or overnight.

120

PEA SALAD I

½ head lettuce, shredded
1 lb. bacon, fried crisp
2 cups cooked peas
6 hard boiled eggs, chopped

½ onion, chopped
2 cups salad dressing
1 cup shredded swiss
cheese

Mix peas, bacon pieces, eggs, onion and salad dressing. Spread on top of lettuce and sprinkle with cheese.

PEA SALAD II

1 cup cooked, diced potatoes
1 cup frozen peas, thawed
½ cup chopped pickles, opt.
1 hard-cooked egg, chopped
1 cup shredded lettuce

$^1/_3$ lite salad dressing
¼ tsp. dry mustard
¼ tsp. honey
¼ tsp. salt
dash of pepper

Combine salad dressing, mustard, honey, salt and pepper. Add remaining ingredients, all but lettuce and mix gently. Chill serve over lettuce.

PEA AND HAM SALAD

1 pkg. frozen peas, thawed
1 cup cooked ham
½ cup chopped onion
¼ cup chopped dill pickles

3 hard boiled eggs,
chopped
1 cup lite salad dressing

Mix all together. Chill and serve.

121

CAULIFLOWER PEA SALAD

Mix together:

1 head cauliflower, diced	1 tsp. salt
1 pint frozen peas, uncooked	1 sm. onion, chopped

Dressing:

1 cup lite salad dressing	½ tsp. pepper
2 tsp. seasoned salt	

Thin with 1 tsp. milk if dressing is too thick. Flavor is better if it sits awhile.

SAUERKRAUT SALAD

1 qt. sauerkraut (rinse in 1 qt. water)
Mix together:

¾ cup fructose	½ cup celery, chopped
½ cup gr. peppers, chopped	½ cup vinegar
pepper and pimento for color	½ cup oil

Pour over sauerkraut and mix.
Note: If using sugar to replace fructose, use 1½ cups.

TACO SALAD

Brown together:

1 lb. ground beef	1 chopped onion

Stir in:

2 cups pork and beans, drain	1 tsp. salt
½ tsp. pepper	

Combine in lg. bowl:

1 cup shredded cheddar cheese	1 head lettuce, torn up
½ bag taco chips, crumbled	2 tomatoes, diced

Toss all together. Serve with taco sauce or french dressing.

OVERNIGHT COLESLAW

1 head cabbage, chopped   1 gr. pepper (can use half
1 onion   red)
Dressing:
¾ cup oil   ¼ cup fructose
½ cup honey

Bring to boil and pour on cabbage while hot. Refrigerate overnight.
Note: If using sugar to replace fructose, use ½ cup.

GERMAN POTATO SALAD

1 cup celery, diced   ⅔ cup vinegar
1 cup onion, diced   ⅓ cup fructose
1 cup bacon, chopped   ½ tsp. pepper
3 tsp. salt   1 ⅓ cups water
8 cups potatoes, cooked, sliced   3 T. flour

Fry bacon,drain. Return 4 T. fat to skillet. Add celery, onion, salt
and flour. Cook gently. Add fructose, vinegar, pepper and water. Bring to a boil. Pour over potatoes and bacon. Pour into 3
qt. baking dish. Cover and **bake at 350 degrees 30 minutes.**
Serves 12.
Note: If using sugar to replace fructose, use ⅔ cup.

1000 ISLAND DRESSING I

2 cups lite salad dressing   2 T. relish
2 T. minced onion   3 T. ketchup
2 hard cooked eggs, minced   milk to taste

Mix all together and thin with a little milk if desired.

THOUSAND ISLAND DRESSING II

3 oz. cream cheese, soft
1 cup lite mayonnaise
3 T. lemon juice or vinegar
            weakened
2 T. relish, sugar free

1 hard boiled egg,
            chopped
¼ cup catsup
⅛ cup fructose

Mix all ingredients. Chill before using.
Note: If using sugar to replace fructose, use ¼ cup.

FRENCH DRESSING I

2 T. grated onion
2 tsp. salt
1 cup canola oil
4 T. lemon juice

2 T. fructose
4 T. vinegar
1 cup ketchup
2 tsp. paprika

Blend all in blender.
Note: If using sugar to replace fructose, use 4 T.

FRENCH DRESSING II

1 sm. onion, grated
¼ cup fructose
½ cup catsup
½ tsp. pepper

1 tsp. salt
1 tsp. worcestershire sauce
¾ cup oil
¼ cup vinegar

Mix first 6 ingredients. Add oil and vinegar slowly. Beat well.
Note: If using sugar to replace fructose, use ½ cup.

Before you flare up at anyone's faults,
take time to count ten of your own.

LETTUCE DRESSING

4 T. onion
4 tsp. salt
¾ cup fructose
4 cups lite salad dressing

8 tsp. mustard
16 T. milk
4 tsp. vinegar

Mix all together. Stores well in refrigerator. Can also use for potato salad.
Note: If using sugar to replace fructose, use 1¾ cup.

COLE SLAW DRESSING

½ cup fructose
½ cup vinegar
1 cup oil
1 tsp. salt

1 tsp. dry mustard
1 sm. onion, diced
1 tsp. celery seed

Beat together until creamy. Store in covered pint jar in refrigerator. Keeps well.
Note: If using sugar to replace fructose, use 1 cup.

CABBAGE SLAW DRESSING

1 pint lite salad dressing
¼ cup vinegar
½ T. salt
dash of pepper

¼ cup oil
dash of celery salt
¼ cup fructose
dash of onion salt

Mix together and store in refrigerator.
Note: If using sugar to replace fructose, use ½ cup.

TOSSED SALAD DRESSING

2 T. honey
¼ cup lemon juice

½ cup canola oil
salt and pepper to taste

Blend all in blender.

SALAD DRESSING I

4 eggs, beaten
1 heaping T. flour
1 tsp. salt
1 cup milk

½ cup fructose
1 cup vinegar
1 tsp. mustard

Mix in order given. Be sure to add milk last and cook until thick.
After cool add 1 pint lite salad dressing.
Note: If using sugar to replace fructose, use 1 cup.

SALAD DRESSING II

2 cups lite salad dressing
½ cup oil
½ tsp. salt

½ cup vinegar
¼ cup fructose
¾ T. mustard

Mix together and use on potato salad.
Note: If using sugar to replace fructose, use ½ cup.

COOKED SALAD DRESSING

⅛ cup fructose
¼ cup flour
2 tsp. salt
2 tsp. dry mustard

1½ cup milk
½ cup vinegar
1 egg, beaten
2 T. butter

Combine fructose, flour, salt and mustard. Add milk and vinegar. Cook on low heat until thickened. Beat egg and add half of top mixture. Mix all together and cook 1-2 minutes. Add butter. This is good on potato salad.
Note: If using sugar to replace fructose, use ¼ cup.

VINEGAR AND OIL DRESSING

½ cup vinegar   ¼ cup fructose
⅓ cup oil   ½ tsp. salt
¼ cup water

Mix well. Pour over salad
Note: If using sugar to replace fructose, use ½ cup.

BLENDER MAYONNAISE

Blend in blender:
2 eggs   1½ tsp. salt
1 tsp. dry mustard   ½ tsp. paprika
2 T. lemon juice

Blend on low and slowly pour in ½ cup canola oil. Add 2 T. vinegar. With blender running add 1½ cup canola oil.

Miscellaneous

Notes

_____

_____

_____

_____

_____

_____

_____

_____

_____

_____

_____

GRANOLA

Combine:

2 cups whole wheat flour

1 cup unsweetened coconut

Combine:

½ cup water

1 cup oil

1 cup honey

6 cups quick oats

1 cup wheat germ

2 tsp. vanilla

1 tsp. salt

Combine all and mix well. Spread on 2 greased cookie sheets. **Bake at 250 degrees 1 hour.**

GLAZED RAISINOLA

4 cups quick oats

1 cup unsweetened coconut

1 cup butter

½ cup honey

2 cups raisins

½ cup slivered almonds

1 cup wheat germ

1 c. raw sunflower seeds

½ tsp. salt

Combine oats, coconut, wheat germ, sunflower seeds and almonds. Melt together butter, honey, and salt. Pour over dry ingredients mixing well. Spread in jelly roll pans. **Bake at 300 degrees 20-30 minutes until golden brown,** stirring several times. Remove from oven and add raisins while still hot.

PANCAKES

1¼ cup flour

¾ tsp. salt

½ cup oil

2 eggs

1 tsp. honey

1½ T. baking powder

1 cup milk

Beat eggs slightly. Add oil and milk. Add dry ingredients. Beat only until flour is mixed. May add blueberries. For waffles add a little more milk.

PANCAKES OR WAFFLES

1 cup cottage cheese
4 eggs
½ cup flour
¼ tsp. salt

¼ cup canola oil
½ cup milk
½ tsp. vanilla

Blend in blender 1 minute. Fry on hot oiled griddle or waffle iron.

OATMEAL PANCAKES

1 egg, beaten
2 T. oil
1 cup buttermilk
1 cup flour
½ tsp. soda

½ tsp. salt
¼ cup fructose
1 T. molasses
½ c. plus 2 T. quick oats

Combine all together and fry on hot oiled griddle.
Note: If using sugar to replace fructose, use ⅓ cup brown sugar and omit molasses.

PUMPKIN PANCAKES

2 cups flour
1 T. fructose
½ cup cooked, mashed pumpkin
1 T. baking powder
1 tsp. salt
1 tsp. cinnamon

¼ tsp. ginger
1½ cups milk
1 T. molasses
1 egg
2 T. oil
¼ tsp. nutmeg

Combine dry ingredients. In separate bowl combine rest of ingredients. Mix all together and fry on hot griddle.
Note: If using sugar to replace fructose, use 2 T. brown sugar and omit molasses.

GOLDEN CRISP WAFFLES

3 eggs
1 T. fructose
½ tsp. salt
½ cup oil

2 cups flour
4 tsp. baking powder
1½ cups milk
1 tsp. vanilla

Beat eggs, add oil and milk, then dry ingredients. Bake on waffle iron.

PUMPKIN NUT WAFFLES

2 cups sifted cake flour
4 tsp. baking powder
1 tsp. salt

¾ tsp. cinnamon
¼ tsp. nutmeg

Mix all together. Separate 3 eggs. Beat yolks with 1¾ cup milk, ½ cup melted shortening, ½ cup pumpkin and ¾ cup chopped pecans. Add dry ingredients. Fold in beaten egg whites. Bake on hot waffle iron.

FRUIT SYRUP FOR PANCAKES

Combine:
¼ cup fructose   3 T. cornstarch
Add: 2 cups water
Bring to a boil, stirring constantly.
Add: 2 cups sliced fresh peaches

Simmer until tender. Add 2 T. lemon juice. Serve hot with pancakes.
Note: If using sugar to replace fructose, use ½ cup.

PINEAPPLE SAUCE FOR PANCAKES

Melt: 3 T. butter
Add:
1 cup crushed pineapple   ½ tsp. molasses
1 T. fructose

Heat 5 minutes, stirring until thick and clear. Use hot or cold on pancakes.
Note: If using sugar to replace fructose, use 2 T. brown sugar and omit molasses.

QUICK FRIED MUSH

1 cup cornmeal   1 cup boiling water
½ tsp. salt   1 T. flour

Combine flour, cornmeal and salt in bowl. Add boiling water and stir well. Drop by spoonfuls into hot skillet. If too thick, add more water.

CORNMEAL MUSH I

Bring to boil 2¾ cups water. Combine 1 cup cornmeal, 1 cup cold water, 1 tsp. salt and ½ tsp. honey; gradually add to boiling water, stirring constantly. Cook until thick. Cover and cook over low heat 10-15 minutes. Pour into loaf pan. Cool. Chill several hours or overnight. Turn out. Slice in ½" or less slices. Fry slowly in hot oil, turning once. Serve with butter or syrup.

CORNMEAL MUSH II

5½ cups water   1¾ cup cornmeal
1 cup cold milk   1½ tsp. salt

Heat water to boiling. Stir in rest of ingredients. Put on lid and let simmer 15 minutes. Pour into bread pans and refrigerate. When set cut in slices and fry.

CORNMEAL SCRAPPLE

3½ cup water
1½ cups cornmeal
⅓ cup flour

1½ tsp. salt
1½ cups cold water

Boil 3½ cups water. Mix together remaining ingredients and add to boiling water. Stir with wire whisk. When thickened add ¾ cup raw ground pork or beef. Stir well. Put in double boiler and cook slowly 2 hours. Pour into loaf pan and chill 12 hours. Slice and fry.

PUMPKIN BUTTER

2 cups pumpkin
⅓ cup fructose
1 T. molasses

¼ cup honey
1 T. lemon juice
¼ tsp. cinnamon

Combine all in saucepan and mix well. Bring to boil on medium high heat, stirring often. Reduce heat and simmer 20 minutes until thickened. Can freeze, can or keep in refrigerator.
Note: If using sugar to replace fructose, use ⅔ cup brown sugar and omit molasses.

APRICOT JAM

16 oz. dried apricots
2½ cups orange juice
½ cup fructose

1 T. lemon juice
½ tsp. cinnamon
¼ tsp. ginger

Combine apricots, orange juice and fructose. Cover and simmer 30 minutes. Mix in lemon juice, cinnamon and ginger. Remove from heat and cool. Blend in blender until smooth. Refrigerate or freeze.
Note: If using sugar to replace fructose, use ¾ cup.

BLACKBERRY JAM (SEEDLESS)

1 12oz. pkg. frozen blackberries ¼ cup fructose
1½ cups white grape juice 1 T. unflavored gelatin

Blend together blackberries and juice. Strain through sieve to get seeds out. Add fructose and bring to a boil. Dissolve gelatin in a little juice. Add to blackberries and remove from heat. Cool to thicken.
Note: If using sugar to replace fructose, use ½ cup. Raspberries may be used in place of blackberries.

CHERRY-RHUBARB JAM

5 cups rhubarb, finely cut 1 can lite cherry pie filling
1 cup water 2 pkgs. (3oz.) sugar-free
2½ cups fructose cherry jello

Cook rhubarb in water until tender. Add fructose and cook a few minutes, stirring constantly. Add pie filling and cook 6-8 minutes. Remove from heat and add jello. Stir until dissolved. Pour into jars and seal.
Note: If using sugar to replace fructose, use 4 cups or to taste.

PEACH JAM

4 cups fresh peeled, chopped 1 T. lemon juice
        peaches ½ tsp. cinnamon
2 cups orange juice 2 T. unflavored gelain,
½ cup fructose dissolved in a little water

Blend or mash peaches and juices. Add fructose. Bring to a boil. Add gelatin and simmer 10-15 minutes. Add cinnamon and chill to thicken.
Note: If using sugar to replace fructose, use ¾ cup. If to thick, may add a little orange juice and blend in blender. If too thin more gelatin may be added.

HOMEMADE MIRACLE WHIP

1 egg plus water to make ¾ cup   ½ tsp. mustard
¾ cup oil   ⅔ cup flour
scant ¼ cup fructose   1 cup water
2 T. salt   ½ cup vinegar

Blend egg and water in blender. Add oil, fructose, salt and mustard. Blend well. In a pan combine flour, water and vinegar. Cook until very thick and add to ingredients in blender. Blend until smooth. Makes about 1 qt.
Note: If using sugar to replace fructose, use ½ cup.

WHIPPED TOPPING

Chill small mixer bowl and beaters several hours before using.
Put in small bowl:
½ cup ice water(may be chilled in bowl)
½ cup dry milk solids
Beat at high speed until peaks form.
Add: 2 T. lemon juice
Beat in gradually: 2 T. fructose
Chill 1 hour.

APPLE PIE FILLING

Peel and slice apples. Fill qt. jars tightly. Cover with syrup. Process 20 minutes in water bath.
Syrup:
2¼ cups fructose   1 cup cornstarch
2 tsp. cinnamon   10 cups water
1 tsp. salt

Cook syrup until thick and bubbly. Add 3 T. lemon juice.
Note: If using sugar to replace fructose, use 4½ cups.

PICKLED RED BEETS

Cook and peel beets and dice in jars.
Syrup:

2 cups vinegar	2 cups water
3 tsp. salt	¼ cup fructose

Make syrup hot and pour over beets. Seal and water bath 15-20 minutes. Makes 8 pints.
Note: If using sugar to replace fructose, use ½ cup.

SWEET DILL PICKLES

1 qt. cider vinegar	onion, opt.
2 cups water	cucumbers
2 cups fructose	dill
½ cup salt	alum

Combine vinegar, water, fructose and salt. Bring to a boil. Place dill in bottom of each jar, slice onion and cucumbers in each jar. Sprinkle in ¼ tsp. alum in each jar. Pour hot vinegar mixture over all and seal. Makes 4 qts.
Note: If using sugar to replace fructose, use 4 cups.

FROZEN CUCUMBERS

2 qts. sliced cucumbers   1 lg. onion
2 T. salt sprinkled over above. Let stand 2 hours; drain.
Mix:
¾ cup fructose   ½ cup white vinegar
Pour over cucumbers and freeze.
Note: If using sugar to replace fructose, use 1½ cups.

138

SALSA

1 gal. tomatoes, peeled, quartered	4 onions, diced
4-6 green peppers, diced	2 T. salt
4-7 hot peppers	¾ cup fructose
1 or more cans tomato paste	½ cup vinegar

Cook slow and bring to boil, simmer 1-2 hours. Add tomato paste after rest is cooked. Put in jars and waterbath 15-20 minutes.
Note: If using sugar to replace fructose, use 1½ cups.

BARBECUE SAUCE

2 tsp. worcestershire sauce	1 cup ketchup
2 T. lemon juice	1 T. salt
½-1 tsp. hot pepper sauce	2 T. cider vinegar
⅛ cup fructose	1 bay leaf
½ T. molasses	½ cup water
2 tsp. mustard	1 clove garlic (minced)

Combine all in small saucepan; bring to boil, stirring occasionally. Reduce heat and simmer 30 minutes. Discard bay leaf. Makes 1½ cups.
Note: If using sugar to replace fructose, use ¼ cup brown sugar and omit molasses.

GLAZE FOR HAM

¾ cup honey	1 tsp. mustard
¾ cup lemon juice	

Combine all and cook until thick. Spread over ham before it's finished baking about 45 minutes.

CHEESE BALL

½ tube soft smoked cheese   8oz. cream cheese
¼ tsp. garlic salt   1 tsp. onion flakes
1 tsp. worcestershire sauce   ½ tsp. seasoned salt
1 pkg. dried beef, shredded   1 tsp. dried parsley

Mix all together. Make into ball. Chill in freezer 1 hour. Roll in parsley.

CHEESE SAUCE

4 T. butter   2 cups milk
4 T. flour   ½ lb. shredded cheddar
1 tsp. salt   cheese

Melt butter. Add remaining ingredients and cook until thickened, stirring constantly. Add cheese and heat until melted.

CHEESE DIP I

1 lg. cottage cheese   1 8oz. pkg. cream cheese
1 cup velveeta cheese   1 tsp. seasoning salt
1/8 tsp. garlic salt

Mix together in blender. Good with chips or vegetables.

CHEESE DIP II

1 lg. pkg. cream cheese   1 T. onion, chopped
1 pkg. dried beef, chopped fine   1tsp. worcestershire sauce

Soften cream cheese and add remaining ingredients. Pour into small baking dish and **bake at 200 degrees 1 hour.** Serve with chips.

140

NACHO CHEESE DIP

8oz. cream cheese
1 can refried beans

1 can Hormel chili
1 pkg. colby jack cheese

Soften cream cheese and spread into 9"x13" pan. Add chili, then beans and spread cheese on top. **Bake at 325 degrees until heated through.** Eat with taco chips.

CHILI DIP

1-1½ lbs. hamburger
2 T. green pepper, chopped
2 T. onion, chopped
1 pkg. chili seasoning

6 oz. tomato paste
3 oz. cream cheese
1 cup water

Brown hamburger, pepper and onion; drain. Add chili seasoning, tomato paste, cream cheese and water.   Simmer ½ hour. Serve with taco chips.

CORNED BEEF DIP

1 8oz. pkg. softened cream cheese
¾ cup plain low-fat yogurt
¾ cup shredded swiss cheese
5 oz. thinly sliced, cooked corned beef

½ cup sauerkraut
$1/8$ tsp. garlic powder

Mix all together until thoroughly blended. Serve with crackers or chips.

COTTAGE CHEESE DIP

Blend in blender:
2 cups cottage cheese
2 T. chopped onion

salt and pepper to taste

Use with crackers or raw vegetables.

SOUR CREAM DIP

8oz. sour cream
1 cup lite mayonnaise
1 T. parsley flakes

1 T. shredded onions
1 T. dill seed
½ T. seasoned salt

Mix together and refrigerate.

BEAN AND BACON DIP

1 cup sour cream
½ cup cheddar cheese, shredded

2 T. dry taco seasoning
1can bean and bacon soup

Combine all in a qt. bowl. Microwave on high 2 minutes and 25 seconds, stirring once. Serve with nacho chips.

CARMEL DIP FOR APPLES

1 cup fructose
2 cups cream
1 tsp. vanilla

1¾ cups white syrup
1 cup butter

Cook fructose, syrup, butter and 1 cup cream together. When boiling, add other cup of cream very slowly. Do not allow to cease boiling. Cook 5 minutes. Add vanilla. Use for dipping apple slices.
Note: If using sugar to replace fructose, use 2 cups.

HONEY PEANUT SPREAD

⅔ cup quick oats
½ cup honey

1¼ cups peanut butter

Toast oats on ungreased pan at 350 degrees 10 minutes.
Cool and combine with honey and peanut butter. Good on sandwiches, celery or fruit slices.

142

SOFT BUTTER SPREAD

Blend together 1 cup butter and ¾ cup canola oil until smooth. Use on bread.

FRIED MOZZARELLA STICKS

16 oz. mozzarella cheese cubes
3 eggs, beaten
¼ cup flour

$^2/_3$ cup fine dry bread crumbs
¼ cup oil

Dip cheese cubes in eggs, then flour, then eggs again and then in bread crumbs. Refrigerate 1 hour. In skillet heat oil and fry until light brown (2-2½ minutes) Drain on paper towels.

SOFT TACO SHELLS

½ cup cornmeal
1 cup flour
1½ cups water

1 egg
1 tsp. salt

Mix all together and fry in a nonstick skillet.

FLOUR TORTILLAS

Combine:
2 cups flour   1 tsp. salt
Cut in: ¼ cup shortening
Add: ½ cup warm water

Knead until smooth. Can refrigerate 4-24 hours before rolling out. Let return to room temperature before rolling out. Divide into 10 balls and roll as thin as possible. Drop onto ungreased very hot griddle. Fry on both sides about 20 seconds.

NOODLES

3 eggs   1 tsp. salt
1 T. milk   flour

Combine all ingredients and add enough flour to make a stiff dough. Divide dough in half rolling out each piece until very thin. When dry cut in thin strips. Store in plastic bags in freezer.

HOMEMADE NOODLES

$3^1/_8$ -$3^1/_4$ cups flour $^1/_3$ cup milk
1 cup egg yolks $^1/_4$ tsp. salt

Sift flour and salt into mixing bowl and form a well. Place eggs and milk inside of well and beat lightly. Gradually mix flour and egg batter by hand. When dough mixture becomes stiff and can be rolled out, turn onto lightly floured board and knead. Roll very thin on floured board, let dry 20 minutes, roll up and cut into $^1/_4$" strips. Unroll. Spread out and let dry 2 hours. Freeze or store in container until needed.

CRACKER JACK

2 sticks oleo $^1/_2$ tsp. soda
$^1/_2$ cup fructose   1 tsp. vanilla
1 T. molasses   8 qts. salted popcorn
$^1/_2$ cup light karo   peanuts, opt.

Cook together 5 minutes. Remove from heat and add soda and vanilla. Pour over popcorn. Add peanuts and mix well. **Bake at 250 degrees $^1/_2$ hour.** Stir every 15 minutes.
Note: If using sugar to replace fructose, use 1 cup brown sugar and omit molasses.

144

LEMONADE

¾ cup lemon juice   1 cup fructose
8 cups water

Stir and chill. Regulate amount of fructose or sugar to taste.

ORANGE JULIUS

²/₃ cup orange juice concentrate   1 cup water
1 tsp. vanilla   1 T. fructose
1 cup milk   10-12 ice cubes

Blend all together in blender.
Note: If using sugar to replace fructose, use 2 T.

APPLE-ORANGE PUNCH

2 qts. cold cider   6 cups sparkling water
2 cans frozen orange juice concentrate

Mix orange juice concentrate into cider, stirring well. Just before
serving add water. Pour into punch bowl over ice cubes and
garnish with oranges.

ORANGE-STRAWBERRY SLUSH

1 (10oz.) pkg. frozen strawberries   ½ cup milk
2 cups orange juice   2 cups ice cubes
½ T. fructose, opt.

Combine all but ice cubes in blender. Blend until smooth. Add
ice cubes and blend until desired consistency.

CIDER JULEP

4 cups cider   1 cup pineapple juice
1 cup orange juice   ¼ cup lemon juice

Mix ingredients and serve with ice in tall glasses.

GRAPE JUICE TO CAN

1 cup grapes   ¼ cup fructose
boiling water

In each jar put 1 cup grapes and fructose. Fill with boiling water.
Put on lids and process 20 minutes.
Note: If using sugar to replace fructose, use ½ cup.

HOMEMADE YOGURT

Scald desired amount of milk. Let cool to 115 degrees. Add 1 T.
plain boughten yogurt (not expired) per qt. Stir briefly. Pour into
jars and place immediately in kettle of water which is 117 degrees. Cover and put in a draft free place. Cover with 1 or 2
towels to keep water warm. Let set about 4 hours or until thick.
May sweeten as desired or add fruit. Refrigerate.

SNOW ICE CREAM

1 cup cream   ¼ cup fructose
1 tsp. vanilla

Mix, then add snow to taste.
Note: If using sugar to replace fructose, use ½ cup.

HOMEMADE PLAY DOUGH

1 cup flour	1 cup water
½ cup salt	1 tsp. cream of tartar
1 T. oil	food coloring

Mix all together well and stir while cooking over low heat. When mixture pulls away from pan, forms a ball and no liquid remains, turn out onto waxed paper and knead until cool. Store in airtight container.

HOMEMADE PAINT

1 tsp. water	½ tsp. food coloring
1 tsp. dishwashing liquid	

Mix all together. Wear an apron or old clothes.

FINGER PAINT

3 T. cornstarch	¾ cup boiling water
2 T. cold water	food coloring

Mix cornstarch and cold water until smooth. Add boiling water. Mix and let cool. Add coloring.

PLANT FOOD

Stir into 1 gallon tepid water:

1 tsp. baking powder	½ tsp. household
1 tsp. salt peter	ammonia

Do not use more often than every 4-6 weeks for watering plants or the leafy ones may crowd you out. Flowering ones may bloom themselves to death.

Fruit and Fruit Juice Sweetened Section

Notes

_____

_____

_____

_____

_____

_____

_____

_____

_____

_____

_____

_____

PUMPKIN DATE BREAD

¹/₃ cup butter
2 eggs
2 T. frozen apple juice
1 cup mashed pumpkin
1½ cups flour
½ tsp. ginger
¼ tsp. cloves
½ cup chopped dates

1 tsp. baking powder
1 tsp. soda
1½ tsp. cinnamon
½ tsp. nutmeg
¼ tsp. salt
½ cup buttermilk
1 cup quick oats

Cream butter and apple juice. Beat in eggs and pumpkin. Combine dry ingredients and add to creamed mixture alternately with buttermilk. Stir in oats and dates. Pour into greased loaf pan. **Bake at 350 degrees 60-70 minutes.** Cool 10 minutes in pan. Remove to wire rack.

GRAHAM CRACKER PIE CRUST

10 graham crackers (crushed fine)
2 T. melted butter   ¼ tsp. sweet 'n low

Combine and press into pie pan. Chill before adding filling.

APPLE PIE I

6 med. apples, peeled, sliced
1 6oz. can frozen apple juice
1½ T. cornstarch
¹/₃ cup water

1 tsp. cinnamon
pastry for 9" double pie
                    crust
3 T. butter

Place apples and apple juice in saucepan. Bring to boil, reduce heat and simmer 5 minutes. Dissolve cornstarch in water and stir into apples. Bring to a boil, reduce heat and simmer 10-15 minutes. Stir in cinnamon. Fill pastry lined pan with apples and top with top crust. **Bake at 350 degrees 45 minutes.** Baste with melted butter.

151

APPLE PIE II

1 6oz. can frozen apple juice
1 lb. apples, peeled, sliced
dash of cinnamon

2 T. cornstarch
dash of salt

Partially cook apples. Combine apple juice with cornstarch and add to apples. Add butter, cinnamon and salt. Stir and pour into unbaked pie shell. **Bake at 350 degrees 40-45 minutes.**

BLUEBERRY PIE

12 oz. fresh or frozen blueberries
Glaze:
2 cups apple juice
2½ T. cornstarch

1 baked pie shell

1 T. lemon juice
½ cup blueberries

In saucepan mix cornstarch, apple juice and ½ cup berries. Cook until thickened. Add lemon juice and remaining berries. Pour into pie shell. Top with whipped cream.

CHERRY PIE

1 double pie crust
4 cups pitted cherries
3 T. quick cooking tapioca
2 T. cornstarch

1 cup frozen apple juice
    concentrate
2 T. butter, melted

Roll out bottom crust and line pie pan. Combine cherries, tapioca, cornstarch, apple juice concentrate and butter. Mix well. Pour into unbaked pie shell. Cover with top crust. **Bake at 400 degrees 10 minutes. Reduce heat to 350 degrees and bake 40-45 minutes longer.**

FRESH PEACH PIE

Crush 3 ripe peaches and add:

3 T. cornstarch   ¼ tsp. cinnamon
¼ c. frozen apple juice concentrate   ¼ cup water

Cook on medium heat until thick and clear. Slice 4 peaches into 9" baked pie crust. Pour slightly cooled mixture over peaches. Top with whipped cream.

PUMPKIN PIE

1 unbaked pie shell   ½ tsp. salt
2 cups pumpkin   ¾ tsp. cinnamon
2 T. flour   ½ tsp. ginger
2 eggs   ½ cup evaporated milk
½ cup frozen apple juice concentrate

Blend all together in blender until smooth. Pour into pie shell. **Bake at 350 degrees 45-50 minutes.**

RAISIN PIE

1 cup raisins   ½ cup milk
½ cup water   2 egg yolks, beaten
¼ c. frozen apple juice concentrate   1 T. cornstarch
¼ tsp. salt   1 baked pie crust

Cook raisins, water, apple juice and salt. Mix egg yolks, cornstarch and milk and pour into raisins. Cook until thickened. Pour into baked pie crust. Top with meringue made with 2 stiffly beaten egg whites. Brown in oven.

STRAWBERRY PIE

½ cup strawberries
water as needed
4 T. cornstarch
1½ cups apple juice concentrate
2½ cups strawberries

1 graham cracker crust,
baked
1 cup whipping cream,
whipped

Crush ½ cup strawberries and add enough water to make ¾ cup. Add cornstarch and apple juice and cook until thick, stirring constantly. Remove from heat. Place remaining berries in pie crust and cover with glaze. Top with whipped cream.

DATE COFFE CAKE

⅓ cup mashed banana
½ cup butter
3 lg. eggs
1 tsp. vanilla
1¼ cups water
Topping:
⅓ cup chopped dates
⅓ cup chopped walnuts

3 cups flour
1 tsp. soda
2 tsp. baking powder
1½ cups chopped dates

⅓ cup unsweetened
coconut

Beat banana and butter until creamy. Add eggs, vanilla and water and beat. Add dry ingredients and beat well. Stir in 1½ cups dates. Pour into oiled 9"x13" pan. Combine topping ingredients and sprinkle over batter. **Bake at 350 degrees 20-25 minutes.**

A happy home is not one without problems,
but one that handles them with
understanding and love.

APPLESAUCE COOKIES I

2 eggs
1 tsp. vanilla
2 cups applesauce, unsweetened
1 cup whole wheat flour
2 cups oats

½ tsp. salt
1 tsp. cinnamon
½ cup nuts, opt.
1 cup dates, chopped
1 tsp. soda

Mix together eggs, vanilla and applesauce. Set aside. Mix together dry ingredients, stir in first mixture. Mix until smooth. Add dates and nuts. Drop onto cookie sheet and **bake at 325 degrees 15-20 minutes.**

APPLESAUCE COOKIES II

½ cup butter, melted
1½ cups unsweetened applesauce
1 cup raisins
1 egg
1 T. frozen apple juice concentrate

1 tsp. soda
1 tsp. cinnamon
dash of salt
2 cups flour

Bring raisins and apple juice to a boil and cool. Set aside. Mix butter, applesauce, raisins and egg together. Sift dry ingredients with 1 cup flour and add to mixture. Add as much of the rest of flour as needed. Drop on cookie sheets and **bake at 375 degrees 10 minutes.** Freeze extra cookies.

DATE BALLS

2 eggs, beaten
½ lb. dates, chopped
½ cup nuts
½ cup butter

1½ cups rice crispy cereal
1 tsp. vanilla
unsweetened coconut

Combine eggs, butter and dates. Cook on low, stirring constantly. Boil 2 minutes. Remove from heat and add remaining ingredients; cool. Shape into balls. Roll in coconut.

DATE COOKIES I

½ cup melted butter
2 eggs, slightly beaten
1 tsp. vanilla
½ tsp. salt
1 T. frozen apple juice, thawed

¼ tsp. almond flavoring
½ cup chopped dates
½ cup flour
½ c. rice krispies cereal

Melt butter over medium heat. Add eggs, apple juice, vanilla, flavoring, dates and salt. Mix well and cook 3 minutes, stirring constantly. Blend in flour and cook 3 more minutes stirring constantly. Stir in cereal. Mix well. Roll in waxed paper and chill 3-4 hours or overnight. Cut in slices to serve. Can also bake instead of chilling.

DATE COOKIES II

1 cup raisins   1 cup water
½ cup dates, chopped
Combine and boil 3 minutes, stirring constantly.
3 tsp. frozen apple juice concentrate 2 eggs
½ cup butter   1 tsp. vanilla
Cream together and add:
¼ tsp. cinnamon   1 tsp. soda
1 cup flour

Mix all together and beat well. Drop onto greased cookie sheet. **Bake at 350 degrees 10-12 minutes.**

PEANUT BUTTER COOKIES

1¼ cups graham cracker crumbs   2 eggs
¼ cup chunky peanut butter   2 T. milk
sweetner to equal ½ cup sugar   2 tsp. baking powder

Beat all together until smooth. Drop onto cookie sheet. **Bake at 350 degrees 10 minutes**

156

SUGARLESS COOKIES

½ cup chopped apples
1 cup raisins
½ cup chopped dates
1½ cups flour
3 eggs
½ cup shortening

1 tsp. vanilla
1 tsp. soda
½ tsp. salt
1 tsp. cinnamon
1 cup water
½ cup chopped nuts

Boil fruits in water 3 minutes; cool. Add remaining ingredients; mix well. Refrigerate 15 minutes. Drop by teaspoon onto greased sheet. **Bake at 350 degrees 15 minutes.** Do not overbake.

RASPBERRY TURNOVERS

1 cup flour
¼ tsp. salt

½ cup butter
1 3oz. pkg. cream cheese

Mix well and chill 3 hours. Divide dough in half. Let rest 10 minutes. Roll each half into 16" square. Cut out 8 4" circles. Repeat with remaining half. Brush edges of circles with a beaten egg. Place 1 heaping T. of fruit sweetened raspberry preserves in center of each circle. Fold over and press edges to seal. Place on greased sheets and **bake at 350 degrees 20 minutes.** Can use different flavored preserves.

APPLE CRISP

4 cups apples, peeled, cored, sliced
1 cup frozen apple juice, thawed
½ tsp. cinnamon
1 T. quick cooking tapioca

1 cup flour
⅔ cup butter
1 cup rolled oats

Combine apples, apple juice, cinnamon and tapioca. Mix well. Pour into 8"x8" baking dish. Combine flour and butter in small bowl and mix until crumbly. Mix in oats. Sprinkle over apples. **Bake at 375 degrees 30 minutes.**

PEACH COBBLER

Crust:

¼ cup butter
1 cup flour
dash of salt
½ tsp. soda
1½ tsp. baking powder
½ cup frozen apple juice
¼ cup milk

Filling:

1 qt. canned unsweetened peaches with juice, sliced
1 T. lemon juice
2 T. frozen orange juice
¼ tsp. cinnamon

Melt butter in 2 qt. baking dish. Combine flour, salt, baking powder and soda. Add milk and apple juice. Stir well. Pour batter into baking dish over butter, do not stir. Top with peaches and juices. Sprinkle with cinnamon. Do not stir. **Bake at 350 degrees 40 minutes.**

CHEESECAKE

1 8" pie shell or graham cracker crust
2 eggs
⅓ cup frozen apple juice
2 tsp. vanilla
8 oz. cream cheese
¼ cup dry milk
1 T. lemon juice

Combine all ingredients and place in crust. **Bake at 350 degrees 30 minutes.** Cool 1 hour and top with favorite unsweetened thickened fruit.

APPLEBUTTER

14 qt. apples, peeled and sliced
1 can unsweetened crushed pineapple
1 gal. cider
2 T. cinnamon

Cook cider down to ½ gallon. Add apples and cook together. Put through colander to make sauce. Add pineapple and cinnamon. Put in roaster and **bake at 350 degrees 3-6 hours, stirring occasionally.** Pour into pint jars and seal.

QUICK APPLE BUTTER

2 cups unsweetened applesauce   ¼ tsp. allspice
1 tsp. cinnamon   ¹/₈ tsp. cloves
¹/₈ tsp. ginger   ¼ cup frozen apple juice

Combine all ingredients in 1½ qt. saucepan. Bring to a boil and boil 30 minutes, stirring often.

RAISIN-APPLE BUTTER

1 cup seedless raisins   2 T. lemon juice
1 cup unsweetened applesauce   2 T. boiling water
¼ cup frozen apple juice   ½ tsp. cinnamon

Soak raisins in water and juices for 15-20 minutes. Put in blender and blend on medium until smooth. Combine with remaining ingredients and cook over low heat until thick, stirring often.

APRICOT BUTTER

1 lb. dried apricots   1 cup white grape juice
1 cup frozen apple juice   2 T. lemon juice
1 tsp. cinnamon

Soak apricots overnight in juices with enough water to cover. In morning add lemon juice and blend until smooth. Cook on low 8 minutes, stirring constantly. Add cinnamon and simmer 10 minutes. May can or freeze.

Christ is the unseen head of every house,
the unseen guest at every meal,
and the silent listener to every conversation.

PEACH BUTTER

2 cups fresh peaches, chopped
1 cup frozen apple juice
1 tsp. cinnamon

1 cup white grape juice
2 T. lemon juice
1½-2 T. unflavored gelatin

Mash or blend peaches with juices. In saucepan bring mixture to a boil. Add gelatin (dissolved in a little water) and simmer about 10 minutes. Add cinnamon. Chill to thicken.
Note: If mixture is too thick, may add more juice and blend in blender. If too thin, more gelatin may be added.

APRICOT JAM

16 oz. dried apricots
2½ cups orange juice
¼ cup frozen apple juice

1 T. lemon juice
½ tsp. cinnamon
¼ tsp. ginger, opt.

Combine apricots, orange juice and apple juice. Cover and simmer 30 minutes. Mix in lemon juice, cinnamon and ginger. Remove from heat and puree in blender. Refrigerate or freeze.

BREAKFAST JAM

Blend desired amount of fresh fruits, apple, peaches, pears, etc. Add almost equal weight of pitted dates.

BLACKBERRY JAM

1 (12oz.) frozen blackberries
1 T. unflavored gelatin

4 cups white grape juice

Put white grape juice in saucepan and cook down to 1½ cups to make concentrate. Take the 1½ cups concentrated grape juice and blend with blackberries in blender. Strain with sieve to remove seeds. Place in saucepan and bring to boil. Add gelatin which has been dissolved in a little juice or water. Remove from heat and cool to thicken.

RASPBERRY JAM

1 (12oz.) frozen red or black raspberries
4 cups white grape juice   1 T. unflavored gelatin

Put white grape juice in saucepan and cook down to 1½ cups to concentrate it. Take the 1½ cups concentrated grape juice and blend with raspberries in blender. Strain through sieve to get seeds out. Place in saucepan and bring to boil. Add gelatin (dissolved in a little juice or water). Remove from heat and cool to thicken.

KNOX BLOX

3 T. unflavored gelatin   1½ cups fruit juice, boiling
1½ cups cold fruit juice

Sprinkle gelatin over cold juice. Let stand 1 minute then add hot juice and stir until dissolved. Pour into 8" or 9" square pan. Chill until firm. Cut into squares.

JIGGLERS

2½ cups boiling water or   2 lg. pkgs. sugar-free jello
            apple juice

Completely dissolve jello in boiling water or juice. Pour into 13"x9" pan. Chill until firm. Cut in desired shapes. To remove shapes, dip pan in warm water for 15 seconds.

FRUIT GELATIN

1 cup unsweetened fruit juice   ½ T. lemon juice
1 T. unflavored gelatin   1 T. frozen orange juice
1 cup unsweetened cold fruit juice or water.

Combine 1 cup fruit juice and gelatin in saucepan. Heat until dissolved. Remove from heat and add remaining ingredients. May add desired unsweetened fruits. Chill until set.

PINEAPPLE SALAD

1 can unsweetened chunk pineapple
Cook until set:

pineapple juice	2 T. cornstarch
2 eggs, well beaten	½ cup frozen apple juice

Cool and add pineapple, grapes and 1 cup whipped cream.

FLUFFY PINEAPPLE SALAD

1 (20oz.) can unsweetened crushed pineapple

2 T. cornstarch	½ c. usweetened coconut
½ cup chopped nuts	1 cup whipping cream

Drain pineapple, saving juice. Reserve 1 cup pineapple pieces. Put remaining pineapple in blender with juice and cornstarch. Blend well. Pour into pan and thicken over medium heat, stirring constantly. Remove from heat. Add coconut, nuts and pineapple pieces. Cool. Whip cream and fold in.

ORANGE PINEAPPLE SALAD

1 T. unflavored gelatin	1 cup cold water
3 T. frozen apple juice	2 T. frozen orange juice
1 cup drained pineapple chunks	2 oranges, peeled, diced
1 sliced banana	

juice drained from pineapple and water to make 1¼ cups

Combine gelatin, water and apple juice in saucepan. Warm until gelatin is dissolved. Add orange juice, pineapple juice and water. Chill until syrupy. Fold in pineapple, oranges and bananas. Chill until set.

162

BREAKFAST DRINK

3 cups cider
¾ cup grape juice

1½ cups orange juice
¾ cup grapefruit juice

Combine all ingredients and serve.

APPLE ORANGE PUNCH

1 qt. chilled cider
1 can frozen orange juice

3 cups sparkling water

Mix cider and orange juice. Just before serving add sparkling water.

PEACH SHAKES

1 qt. frozen unsweetened peaches
2 cups Dole Orchard Peach juice

Let peaches thaw 10 minutes. Put peaches and juice in blender and blend on high until thick and smooth. Can use other fruits if desired.

SUGARLESS CANNED PEACHES OR PEARS

Wash, peel and remove seeds. Fill qt. jars with fruit halves or slices. For syrup, combine 1 cup unsweetened pineapple juice and 2 cups water. Pour syrup over fruit. Water bath 10 minutes. Note: Other juices may be used instead of pineapple if desired. White grape juice is good.

GRANOLA

2 cups rolled oats
1½ cups wheat germ
½ cup slivered almonds
½ cup unsweetened coconut
¼ cup sesame seeds

½ cup sunflower seeds
1 cup frozen apple juice,
           thawed
½ cup oil

Combine all but apple juice and oil in 9"x13" pan and mix well. Place apple juice in saucepan and bring to a boil. Continue boiling until reduced by half, remove from heat. Add oil and slowly pour over granola mixture. Mix well. **Bake at 250 degrees 1 hour.** Stir every 15 minutes.

MUFFINS

1 egg
1¾ cup flour
1 tsp. baking powder
½ tsp. soda

1 cup sour cream
¼ cup frozen apple juice,
           thawed
½ tsp. salt

Beat together egg, sour cream and apple juice until smooth. Sift remaining ingredients together and add to egg mixture. Stir just until mixed. Fill 12 greased muffin tins ⅔ full. **Bake at 400 degrees 20 minutes.**

FRUIT-NUT MUFFINS

1 cup chopped dates
½ cup raisins
½ cup chopped prunes
½ cup water
½ cup butter, soft
¼ tsp. salt

2 eggs, beaten
1 tsp. vanilla
1 cup flour
1 tsp. soda
½ cup chopped nuts

In saucepan, combine dates, raisins, prunes and water. Bring to a boil and boil 5 minutes. Stir in butter and salt. Set aside to cool. Add remaining ingredients to fruit. Stir just until moistened. Spoon into greased muffin tins. **Bake at 350 degrees 15 minutes.**

Index

BREADS

DESSERTS

FRUIT AND FRUIT JUICE SWEETENED

MAIN DISHES

170

MISCELLANEOUS

SOUPS AND SALADS